THE OTHER SIDE OF SILENCE

THE OTHER SIDE OF SILENCE

A Novel

Pauline Schokman

First published in 2016 by Karnac Books.

This new edition published in 2019 by Sphinx, an imprint of
Aeon Books
12 New College Parade
Finchley Road
London NW3 5EP

British Library Cataloguing in Publication Data

A C.I.P. for this book is available from the British Library

ISBN-13: 978-1-91257-363-9

Typeset by Medlar Publishing Solutions Pvt Ltd, India

www.sphinxbooks.co.uk

For my husband Laurie

with love

"If we had a keen vision and feeling of all ordinary human life, it would be like hearing the grass grow and the squirrel's heart beat, and we should die of that roar which lies on the other side of silence."

—George Eliot, Middlemarch

Louis fingered the neck of his acoustic guitar, his Maton; it always came with him. He was seated on a low couch that ran along one wall of their tiny farmhouse. He glanced up at Anna as she stood in the galley kitchen putting finishing touches to the evening meal. He watched her as she chopped fresh basil and coriander and was caught by the steady rhythm of her knife as it rose and fell. She moved to the stove and tossed a handful of the herbs into one saucepan, then lifted a piece of spaghetti from the next with a fork and chewed slowly, testing to see if it was ready. She seemed absorbed by her task and unaware of him. He leant forward and strummed his guitar loudly. The sound was rasping, discordant. Anna flinched as she turned to face him. Louis smiled as he spoke, his voice eager. "I heard from Charlie yesterday. Just before we set off."

It was Saturday evening. The drive from Melbourne the night before had taken five and a half hours, plenty of time to talk about Charlie, but Louis had slept most of the way. They had both risen late that morning and busied themselves on the property during the day: he mending fences and spreading hay in the paddocks, she sanding back a small cedar table they had brought with them. She looked at him. The light from the standing lamp in the corner played across his dark features as he focused on his instrument once again and she realised that somewhere she still found him attractive. She tensed in anticipation for she could predict what was coming. Perhaps she was wrong. She kept her voice calm, her tone non-committal. "I didn't know he was back in Melbourne."

"He thinks he could line up another tour for me; through New South Wales and Queensland, mostly regional centres. He's got a good support band who are keen." He glanced towards her and his eyes gleamed with excitement as they met hers.

A quiet rage began to well in her. She could feel it gaining momentum. She looked at the brightly coloured salad on the table between them, the carefully laid places, the jug of water and glasses, the absence of the usual bottle of wine that would be open to breathe at this stage in the preparation of the meal. She had convinced herself this month would be different. "Why, Louis? Why tonight?"

"Christ! Here we go!" He stood his guitar against the couch and sat bolt upright. His face tensed. "Spoiling your plans, am I? Might help to let me in on them."

"I asked you a simple question."

"God, that snide voice of yours!"

"Do you want me to say nothing? Really? Is there any way I could say this that would reach you?" He was right. She hated the tone of her voice. She was seething with resentment. She knew if she said anything more it would only make it worse, but if she remained silent in the face of this she would despise herself. "I'm mid-cycle, Louis. You know it. This is the fifth month you've done this."

He stood up and stared at her with undisguised hatred. "Done what exactly?"

"Begun a conversation you know will start a fight. We'll take days to make up. Bingo! Opportunity over!" She was almost shouting.

"Bingo! Bingo?" His tone was mocking. "Annie, you're losing it." He walked across the room towards her and for a moment she felt a strange pang of fear. Why, she had no idea. He had never hurt her physically. He reached forward and grabbed the car keys from where they lay on the bench between them. He headed for the door and picked up his coat on the way out. "I'm off to the pub for a meal. Don't wait up for me!"

She ate her meal in silence and placed the leftover food in bowls to cool before transferring it to the fridge. She washed the dishes and cleaned up in a slow methodical manner. She felt dazed. She curled up on the couch and pulled a blanket over her as she waited for him to return. She heard the car but pretended to be sleeping when he came in. His step was heavy. She knew he had drunk too much as she heard him stumble in the corridor and the bedroom door close. She rose quietly and moved to sit at the table. It was a dark night with no moon and the stillness surrounded her. She listened for, but could not hear, the shrill calls of the sugar gliders that fed nightly in the long line of manna gums down by the river, only 100 metres away.

Then it came, her companion, the low howl of the wind as it circled the little house and rustled the gum trees next to it before heading out across the paddocks. She sat and studied the hands that lay clasped on the table in front of her. In the dim light thrown by the lamp from the far corner of the room they looked strangely old, tired. She could not make herself rise and walk down the corridor to the room where he would be sleeping soundly, as he always did after venting his rage in that way. In the morning he would be surly, would expect her to try to cajole him back into a more amiable mood. It was like a dance with set steps. Why had they come? She had no heart for this any more.

She lifted her head from the table. Her hand was numb. She must have laid her head on it for hours. She walked to the window and pulled the curtain aside. The grey light that was just beginning was not strong enough to make its way into the room. She peered into it but could see nothing. She could not even make out the poles of the fence just by the driveway to the farmhouse. There must be a mist. She let the curtain fall and walked to the rectangular pantry off the kitchen at the back of the house. She chose the smaller of the two pairs of gumboots that stood under the lowest shelf. The shelves, like the room, were painted cream and were laden with an assorted array of biscuits, tinned fruit, unopened jars of jam, pickles, chutneys, boxes of cereals, anything that had a few months at least before its use-by date ran out. She chose a packet of savoury biscuits at random and thrust it into the canvas pack that she lifted off a hook on the wall, together with her dark green waterproof jacket. Lastly she picked up the fishing tackle box and a small pail full of worms off the floor.

She slid on the boots, donned her coat, slipped her gloves onto her hands, then let herself out by the back door. She moved silently, careful to make sure the fly-wire door did not slam behind her. On the square wooden platform that served as a back veranda were several fishing rods leaning against the wall of the house. She took two and walked down the steps to the gravel drive. She trod carefully, but her boots crunched on the moist gravel and she looked up to see a cow raise its head and gaze at her with deep doleful eyes as it stood by the fence. Was it questioning her folly in being out in this by choice? Already the mist was lifting over the paddocks. It lay in wisps in the gullies now and she could see the line of trees in front of her easily as she walked down the sloping drive towards the river. She opened the long metal gate across the drive and slipped through, careful to chain it securely behind her.

She looked back up the hill at the little wooden farmhouse framed by three large gum trees. She loved this place. Its remoteness and the peace it afforded her were something she would never have predicted before they had bought it. She looked along the road; it was narrow at this point and ran alongside the river for several kilometres before ending in the tiny township of Bemm River where the river spilled into the lake. All was silent save for the dawn chorus as the birds woke and piped their greeting to the chill winter morn. She crossed the road and picked her way the short distance along the well-trodden dirt path through the brush and native grasses to the river's edge. Their boat was moored at their makeshift jetty. Louis and she had built it in better times, five years ago; another lifetime.

She climbed into the little boat and it swayed as she made her way along its length. She took a life jacket and large torch from the space beneath the bow. She pulled the jacket on, tied it securely, then moved to the stern, unlocked and lifted the outboard motor towards her and lowered it carefully into the water. She yanked at the pull cord and it spluttered to life but died as rapidly. She waited a moment then tried again. This time it sprang to life and droned noisily. She sat with one hand steering the engine, the other holding the torch as she scanned ahead for snags in the river. It was a slow trip down the river. A white-faced heron stared at her from the river's edge as she passed and cormorants lifted off in front of her to skim the water and land on nearby boughs.

She passed two other boats on opposite sides of the river. The fishermen in them waved her on silently; bream fishermen almost certainly. The river began to widen as it neared its mouth and the line of brush and gum trees on its bank gave way to open paddocks and farmland. Small groups of cattle huddled near the water's edge but none came down to drink. A fish jumped in front of her and the cold air hurt her face. She could not feel her nose as she brushed small icy drops from its end with her woollen glove, yet the cold and the river both enlivened her. She entered the lake and began to steer at a diagonal making for the depths of the channel that in late spring or early summer opened to the mighty Pacific Ocean of its own accord, or was blasted open by the local farmers if the river began to inundate their lands with its spring floods.

On the lake there was a fresh wind. She could make directly for the channel at this time of year. No chance of being grounded on a sandbar as there was in summer. She scanned the lake and counted three other boats dotted around its banks. She entered the mouth of the channel and moored her boat to a large tea tree. Carefully she baited her hook. She heard a high pitched whistle and looked overhead to see a sea eagle on the wing surveying the dunes and bush, circling its territory. An image flashed into her mind, eerie, uninvited: her body lying face upwards on the lake bed, hair streaming out intertwined among the reeds, her eye sockets empty, unseeing, eels swimming over her. No one need know. It would seem like some tragic accident.

A loud fluting call startled her; black swans flying unusually low, in formation, black wings tipped with white outstretched, long necks fully extended in a line ending in the red of their beaks. This was how she liked to see them best, in this place where they seemed wild and free, not gliding gracefully on some ornamental lake in the city for all the poets' accolades that might arouse. She analysed the scene that had flooded her a moment before dispassionately. It was one option, but there was another: a life without Louis.

* * *

He shuffled into the kitchen half-dressed. He had taken his jeans off but slept in his shirt which was crumpled and partly askew. His dark midday stubble was peppered with silver and there was a grey streak in the lock of hair that fell across his forehead and clung to it. She averted her gaze from his long naked legs and underpants as she turned back to the stove. She skilfully flipped the fillets of fish she was frying in a heavy metal frying pan.

"You've been on the river this morning?" There was a note of genuine surprise in his voice.

"Got these in the lake. They're just tailor. I didn't catch anything in the channel, so I tried my luck trawling on the trip back." Had she ever not crawled into bed with him after a fight, not tried to find some way to make it better between them? She couldn't remember such a time.

"So, do you want to stay tonight then? We should shift those cows to the back paddock." He was looking at her keenly.

She could feel his eyes on her but she did not meet them. "No, I can't, I have to get back … I'm fully booked in the morning. I've called the Parsons and let them know. They'll take care of it. We've got to leave by five at the latest." Her tone was matter of fact, businesslike. She kept all emotion out of it. "Here, I've cooked enough for you if you want some. The rest are in the freezer."

She had told him that her father was coming to Melbourne, but had not mentioned that she was meeting him for lunch the next day. Still, he had not asked her what her plans were either. She piled the fish, onion rings, and garlic all fried in butter on the plates in front of her and placed them on the table. She walked to the fridge and pulled out the salad from the day before. She lifted the plastic wrap and crunched into a bit of lettuce, then placed it in the middle of the table and sat down. He watched her uneasily as she slowly began to eat her meal, her eyes never leaving her plate. He pulled his chair out and sat down opposite her. They ate in silence.

* * *

"I've had to squeeze a possible appendix in at ten." Anna met her receptionist's eyes and Mary looked back guiltily. She was in her mid-twenties, blonde, efficient, and eager to please. Anna liked her. "It's Billy Walters. He's six and doesn't want to see any of the others at the best of times."

"Okay, but that's it. I have to get away by one today, Mary. It's important!" She scanned the waiting room. All but two of the beige office chairs that lined the long rectangular room were occupied; two businessmen in suits reading magazines, a young mother with a baby on her lap trying to interest a toddler in a storybook. The mother looked up eagerly as she glanced her way and Anna got no further in her surveillance of the room. She smiled at the woman and looked away.

She lifted the first patient history from her pile. "Emma Rogers." A woman in her early forties stood and moved towards Anna, her smile of recognition contrasting strangely with the sadness in her eyes. Anna glanced briefly at the card in her hands before greeting her patient. It was a bad start. "Hi Emma."

Anna ushered her patient ahead of her. As she did so Don stepped out of his consulting room a few metres away and motioned to her over the patient's head.

"Last room on the right, as usual, Emma. Please take a seat. I'll just be a moment." Anna stood in the door of her colleague's room as she watched her patient walk on further down the corridor to hers.

Don's consulting room was much larger than hers and far messier; piles of paperwork and medical magazines, unopened in their plastic wrappers, filled the bench beside her. The walls were covered with his children's artwork and photos. He was already back behind his desk sifting through some papers in front of him. He was thickset, almost stocky. He must have put on weight. She noted too that his reddish-brown hair was receding. They saw each other most days of the year but when was the last time she had actually seen him?

"Come in, Anna. Shut the door."

She did not move but waited silently until he looked up at her. She raised her eyebrows in obvious annoyance. "So?"

He smiled in a conciliatory way. "Two minutes. I promise."

She shut the door behind her but remained standing next to it.

"Can you cover for me tonight? Joey's in a concert and I completely forgot. Trish will be furious if I don't make it."

She could see he had already assumed she was going to do it. Well, why not? She usually did; the one with no children, the one whose partner was off touring.

"Sorry, Don." Her voice was soft but firm. "I'm not going to be in this afternoon and I'm busy this evening. My Dad's here from New York."

He looked surprised. He fiddled awkwardly with the papers on his desk but made no attempt to talk her into it. "Okay. Sure. I'll see if Bill's free." She turned to go and he seemed to remember her. "You were speaking to your Dad in Sydney last week, weren't you? How long since he's been here?"

"Three years." She hesitated as she reached for the door. She had made no mention of these phone conversations to Louis. The weekend had seemed too important and his relationship with her father was too intense and complex. Well, it had made no difference. She opened the door, steeled herself mentally, and headed for her consulting room.

She shut the door behind her and sat beside her desk which faced the back wall. Her patient sat a metre away, alongside her. The window behind the woman was almost obscured by a large white camellia bush in full bloom, but a surprising amount of light still filtered into the small room. "Yes, Emma, how can I help?" The woman's intense brown eyes stared searchingly into hers. She felt slightly off balance. "Emma?"

"I want a referral for a fallopian tube ligation. I don't want to go back to Margaret Dixon. She'll try to talk me out of it."

"Are you sure? How does Richard feel about it?"

"He's the one who suggested it. Actually he suggested having a vasectomy. But I don't think it's fair on him. He's eight years younger than me. Who knows what's going to happen."

Anna found her mind weighing up all the time she had spent with Emma Rogers: four years and how many tries at

IVF, then a cot death when little Sally was six months old, an unexpected miracle pregnancy last year, followed by a miscarriage two months later.

"Anna, I really can't cope with any more."

"Okay, Emma. But I'm putting your full history on this referral. Did you go and see the grief counsellor I suggested?" She felt like such a hypocrite, she guessed the answer.

Emma's eyes filled with tears. "I can't do it. I'm not ready to talk to anyone." She looked imploringly at Anna, her voice was barely audible. "I'll go mad if I talk about it."

* * *

Despite her best efforts she was late. Only fifteen minutes, but she knew how he would hate it. He would not have left. He was past that sort of thing, with her at least. He would never deign to comment, but somewhere it would wound him, make him feel she did not value him highly enough. It was not the beginning she had wanted. She pulled at her tailored woollen skirt, adjusted her blouse, and ran her fingers though her hair without knowing she was doing any of it, as she hurried towards the glass doors of the restaurant. She had almost been running and felt flustered by the time she reached them. She stood for a moment in front of the doors and took a deep breath. Once on the other side she slowed her pace and walked as calmly as she could as she approached the maître-d'. She did her best not to comb the room with her eyes for her father, still she noticed him at once, at a choice table by the window. He must have been able to see her coming. She flushed with embarrassment.

The maître-d' was a small, spritely man in his fifties. He smiled at her warmly. "Ah, Dr Mason! Your father is expecting you."

She smiled back. "Yes, I know. I hope he hasn't been waiting long."

"I'm sure you know that for the maestro, to wait at all is to wait too long!" His humour was genuine, as was his obvious affection for her father. How did he do it? She could understand the adulation that surrounded him in the musical world but at any restaurant, exhibition, gallery, anywhere she had ever met her father in any country in the world, there was always this sense that he was known, liked, or maybe even loved by some stranger who knew how best to please him. Something she, as his daughter, could clearly never get right.

She slowed her gait as they approached the table.

Her father looked up at her. "So, no Louis?"

Her smile faltered. Her voice sounded young and uncertain as she poured out her confession. "I didn't tell him I was having lunch with you. I wanted some time with you, alone."

"Ah." He leant forward as she bent to kiss him on the cheek. The maître-d' seated her opposite her father, cleared away the third place setting and left. He sat in silence for a moment, appraising her. "You've lost weight, you look …" She struggled to hold his gaze as she waited for his verdict. The pause seemed endless. He smiled slightly and continued. "… almost gaunt. Be careful, my dear, you don't want to lose your beauty."

What, like my mother? She used all that she had not to voice it. This was his way of punishing her for being late, for not bringing Louis.

He picked up the menu and began to hand it to her. "Would you care to have a look?"

"No, Dad. You order." Her chance to make amends in some small way. She pulled her gaze from the pattern of roses on the starched damask tablecloth a few centimetres in front of her plate; they were slightly raised in pure white, yet able still to form a contrast. She met her father's eyes momentarily. "Please. You've had time to decide. Surprise me."

Frederick Mason eased back ever so slightly in his chair; a sense of pleasure emanated from him. A waiter appeared immediately. He deftly unfurled Anna's serviette and placed it on her lap, filled the water glass in front of her from the pear-shaped jug on the table, and hovered just the right distance from her father's side, attentive, deferential. "We'll start with the quail eggs, and then the trout." The waiter's eyes moved to the wine list in surprise. Her father looked at him amused. "No, water will do."

Once the waiter had left he reached into the inner breast pocket of his jacket and pulled out a small, elongated rectangular envelope. He placed it on the table between them and pushed it across to her.

"For you and Louis. Tonight's concert, no excuses. Be prepared, it's a one act affair. I'm far too old for marathons. Afraid they just have to put up with it if they want me."

"They clearly do Dad, and yes, we'd love to come." They would be the very best tickets, they always were, and Louis would come of course. They would charm each other, these two men in her life, so alike, yet so different. "Still just the two concerts in Melbourne?"

"Yes, I fly out to Berlin on Wednesday."

She felt a wave of heaviness. She forced herself to speak. "Are you seeing Chloe?"

"No, no. I don't want to upset her in any way." Chloe and her father always fought, or rather Chloe always found some way to disapprove of him, to challenge, bait, or wound him. Things had only got worse since Chloe had married Adrian, for all her supposed new-found love and generosity. Anna was amazed at her father's consideration. Chloe was a week overdue in her first pregnancy. Anna had been sure that her father's concert tour had been timed to meet his first grandchild. Her chest tightened immediately … no, not his first.

"In any case you know that she and Adrian are staying with your mother." He gave his short harsh laugh, the one reserved solely for reference to her mother and otherwise quite uncharacteristic. "I hardly risk that encounter, even by phone."

She looked at him in pained amazement. He was in his early seventies, her mother in her mid-sixties. They shared two children and a knot of bitterness that seemed to have tightened, if anything, in the twenty-five years since their relationship had ended. They could not be in the same room together and had no way of even speaking. Her mother had never forgiven him his infidelity and he had never forgiven her for her cruelty. Neither had remarried. Chloe was the one to choose who would come to her wedding, who would be there at the birth of her child, or at least she seemed the one who felt compelled to choose. Anna had elected not to marry, and neither parent would ever be trusted at a time of such intimacy as the birth of a child. Was she any freer in these choices?

"Ah, here it is." Her father examined the dish in front of him. She knew he was assessing the composition and contrast of colour and texture and what he saw pleased him. He lifted his fork and knife, ready for the next phase of the encounter. It was how he approached each meal, each moment of the day; he retained all the enthusiasm and disappointment in life of a young child. It was what she most loved and feared about him. She watched him with a kind of awe and reverence as the first carefully selected morsel moved, delicately poised on the end of his fork, and was taken into his mouth with something akin to a caressing action of his lips. She started: she felt annoyed at how quickly and completely a fascination with her father could absorb her even when she thought she was prepared to face him. She looked at the food before her on her plate. She feared it was far too rich for her own taste. She began to emulate his slow thoughtful way of eating; decreasing the contents of her plate gradually in a way that still left balance in what remained.

He smiled at her warmly. "So?"

"It's delicious, Dad. You always choose so well. Not something I would try myself otherwise."

This pleased him. "Why don't you and Louis come and spend Christmas with me at Rhode Island this year? You haven't had a white Christmas since you were in your teens. I'm sure you'd both enjoy it. We could take in some shows on Broadway, go ice skating at the Rockefeller Centre." His eyes held a faraway look.

Was he lonely now? Was there no current lover to help ease his solitude? Did he truly regret his estrangement from her or from Chloe?

"I'll think about it, Dad, and let you know."

"Good, good."

* * *

Anna sat in the departure lounge carefully adjusting the strap of the smart, emerald green bag she was taking with her as hand luggage. The bag had bumped awkwardly against her thigh as she made her way to the lounge. It was not how she wanted him to see her when she disembarked at the other end. She had her black knee-high leather boots and favourite red scarf and gloves packed within. She would don them when they were near their destination. She was bursting with a strange mixture of anticipation, excitement and dread, but more than anything she wanted to appear relaxed and confident. New York, they were flying to New York. She would put up with the indignity of being treated like a child, having to be supervised by some stewardess just because she was not yet eighteen, for the sake of this chance to fly overseas, to visit their father in his home. Anyway it might actually prove helpful to have a stewardess keeping an eye on them if Chloe got out of hand.

Anna looked across at her sister sprawled over two seats a little way away from her, chewing gum and picking at the scabs on her forearm, from where she had forced a pen under her skin a week ago. The thought of it made Anna feel sick. She hoped, more than anything she could remember hoping for, that Chloe would find some way to behave like a normal person so that they could have a chance to get to know their father again. She felt someone's eyes on her and glanced up to find her mother looking at both of them with a deep sense of satisfaction, or some weird kind of pleasure. Anna did not trust it. This trip really made no sense.

In the seven years since their parents separated and then divorced they had only seen their father for a few days or a week at a time, once or twice a year. They would stay with him in an expensive hotel in Melbourne, or fly to Sydney and once to Perth to do the same. This was their first visit to his home in New York and they were due to stay for two weeks. Their mother had forbidden it until now and Anna had not had the courage to defy her. Suddenly, totally unexpectedly, their mother had decided it would be a good thing for them to visit their father and spend Christmas with him.

Felicity Mason took a few steps closer to her daughters, close enough that they could hear her without anyone else doing so. When they had arrived at the departure lounge Chloe had marched to the row of seats furthest away from the staff and the counter, and Anna and her mother had followed. They were very early for the flight and the lounge was only a third or so full. Felicity turned to Anna, dressed in a colour-ful summer top and skirt and earnestly clutching the stylish grey woollen coat that Felicity had lent her. "Don't think that this visit will actually mean anything to him, Anna. If he cared about either of you he'd be here in Australia, not on the other side of the world." Her glance took in Chloe as well. Anna looked studiously in front of her and Chloe seemed totally absorbed as she pulled a thread in her tights and watched a hole grow in them, then looked up and stared out of the large windows at the planes on the tarmac.

"And I expect that coat back exactly as it is. Or you will have to replace it." Felicity laughed mockingly. "Or your darling Daddy will!"

Anna felt a strong compulsion to hand the coat to her mother at once, yet then she would arrive in New York unprepared for winter and her father would need to buy one for her immediately. It was the exact opposite of what she wanted. She was hoping to impress him with how well she could travel, how prepared she was. She did not want to be of trouble to him in any way. She looked down and said nothing.

"Did you hear me, Anna? You'd better acknowledge what I'm saying or you can give me that coat right now."

"I heard you, Mum. You'll get it back just as it is, don't worry."

Chloe sniggered, and drew her mother's attention to her instead.

"Chloe, stop picking at your arm like that! It looks disgusting enough as it is."

Chloe continued to ignore the fact that her mother had spoken and eased the long nail on her right index finger under the edge of the biggest scab on her left forearm. She levered it up in a slow methodical way and blood began to ooze from the wound. Felicity was a tall woman, far taller than her younger daughter. She sprang forward and in a sudden unexpected move grabbed Chloe's wrist, prising her right hand away from her left arm. Chloe shrieked. Many heads turned in their direction and a stewardess left the counter and began to walk their way. Felicity let her daughter's wrist drop immediately. She rummaged in her handbag and brought out a wad of tissues which she handed to Chloe.

"Press that on your arm now and start behaving yourself. Or you can forget about this trip!" She turned to include Anna. "Both of you! I don't care how much he's spent on the flights!"

Anna looked from Chloe to her mother in desperation. "That's completely unfair!"

Her mother glowered down at her, her voice strangely cool. "I don't give a damn, Anna. So if you want to go on this trip you had better keep your sister in line." Her facial expression turned from anger to something much more spiteful. "In fact I'm holding you responsible for Chloe. You're to make sure that she behaves herself properly."

Anna's face fell. She felt nothing but dismay. How was she supposed to do something her mother clearly could not?

* * *

"I'm not going! I don't give a fuck about Tommy! I don't even know who The Who are!" Her voice was full of snide contempt.

"Just give it a try, sweetheart. I'm sure you'll enjoy it." His pleading tone only made it worse.

"You and Annie go lord it up on Broadway, just leave me here. I'll be fine." Chloe glared at him; her intense blue eyes, a copy of his own, bored into him, daring him to take her on.

Frederick looked at his daughter with despair. Her once beautiful golden hair had a bright magenta streak in it and hung in limp, dirty-looking strands beside her thin face. A ring protruded from her left nostril. Her scant bits of clothing were all black or dark purple, and her only footwear seemed to be a pair of heavy leather, calf-length boots. He longed to drop her at the hair salon and take her shopping. He had no idea how to reach her. Most of all he hated her mother. How had Felicity let it come to this?

Anna watched them both from an armchair in the far corner of the room. Not again. They would miss the show, almost certainly. They had left the ice rink at the Rockefeller Centre yesterday when she was finally starting to enjoy herself, having got as far away from Chloe as she possibly could. Chloe was thirteen and in this constant rage, she just wanted to spoil things, always. It was her way of relating to the world. Anna was sick of it. She wished more than anything that Chloe had stayed at home. There was no chance really to see how

17

their father lived, to find out who he was here, what kept him on the other side of the world from them. There was no time for anything but Chloe's foul moods and her opposition to anything he had planned that they might enjoy together. Even worse, Chloe was constantly on the phone, complaining to their mother, making out that everything was awful here, behaving as though she missed her terribly. Why? Anna could not fathom it. At home all Chloe did was bag their mother and talk endlessly about how much she hated living with her.

"Chloe, Silvia is coming with us tonight. I want you to meet her. It's important to me." He turned to include Anna in the conversation. "Annie, come over here please."

Anna rose slowly and walked the few steps to his side with a sense of dread, not at what he might tell her; he had already told them that he was serious about Silvia. The thought of him happy with someone other than their mother gave her hope. Had her mother somehow guessed that there was someone he truly cared for in his life? He would never tell her directly, but perhaps she knew him well enough to sense it in his mood, in some subtle thing he revealed while negotiating with her for access to his children. Had they been sent with a purpose? For what she feared was Chloe's reaction and the mayhem she might cause in his life. Anna wished she could protect him, prevent it somehow, but she had no idea what to do. She stood as close to him as she dared. She wanted to take his hand, whether to give or receive reassurance she was not quite sure, but it was not something that she could do or that she imagined he would allow. She consoled herself with his proximity.

Chloe glared at them, enraged. "Christ, you're pathetic, Anna! Acting like his doting little girl. You're sixteen for fuck's sake! He barely ever sees us. Stop trying to play happy families!"

"Shut up, Chloe! Just shut your mouth for once! You don't want anyone to be close. All you ever do is ruin things for us."

"Anna, please don't talk to your little sister that way." Her father was looking at her with shock and concern.

She stared at him, incredulous. "What?" She shook her head slowly from side to side. She glanced at Chloe who was smirking at her triumphantly.

The doorbell rang and Frederick walked slowly to the door of his apartment. He opened it, and halted to kiss the woman standing there, before he ushered her in. She was not what Anna had envisaged at all. She had imagined someone young, blonde, and pretty. Silvia was at least their father's age, perhaps a little older, stately and serious, and quite beautiful in an unusual, unconventional way; her features lacked symmetry: her eyes and her mouth were too large, and yet somehow they worked. She smiled at Anna with what seemed like genuine warmth and Anna smiled back. If only such a thing were possible.

Chloe started laughing hysterically. "She looks like a fucking clown!"

* * *

The trout came and it was delicious. Anna ate it with relish. She savoured each mouthful. She wished there was more she could say, but maybe this was enough; to remember a meal that they had, in the end, enjoyed together. If Louis were here her father and he would talk music, a language so familiar to her and yet one in which she had no ability to communicate. She would be relegated to spectator, audience, listener. It was one of the reasons she had chosen not to bring Louis. Her father ordered chocolates and coffee. Soon this meal would be over. He had not asked one question about her, her work, how she was coping this hardest of years. Was that what she had hoped for in coming alone? She felt the pressure of tears welling unbidden behind her eyes. She looked down and fought to keep them back.

"Yes, Anna, you must come to me for Christmas. You're far too glum, my dear. Louis and I will cheer you up together." The meal was over, he was signalling for the bill. They rose in silence and walked out together.

"Do you need a lift, Dad? I'm parked close by."

"No, no. I'll walk. My hotel's not far at all. I need a stroll in the sunshine before I get ready for tonight. You will come backstage?"

"Of course, Dad, of course we will."

TWO

"I hope you realise that I'm doing this for Fred!" He pulled on his jacket as she fastened her earrings.

"Don't worry, I took that as given." She looked in the dressing table mirror to apply her lipstick and could see him behind her, glaring at her. He still spruced up so well. He must have noted the desire in her eyes, even though he could only see it in the mirror. He was instantly behind her and pulled her against him. They both gazed at their combined reflection, his arm around her waist, his mouth nuzzling her neck. The emerald green of her dress accentuated the creamy pallor of her skin and the darkness of her hair. It was a taffeta cocktail dress; classic in design it draped seductively over her cleavage without being too revealing, then tapered at her waist and outlined the fullness of her hips. Would her father call her gaunt in this?

"You look gorgeous in that dress. I could ravish you."

She pulled away from him abruptly. This was so much a part of their relating, something she had taken years to see; the offer of what she wanted at the expense of something else that was important to her.

"There's no time for that now. We've got to get a move on as it is."

"You can be a harsh bitch, Anna. Watch out, or you'll end up just like your mother."

Her worst fear, his ultimate barb, usually used sparingly with utmost care and timed to cause maximum impact, yet tonight spoken so freely with no build-up preceding it. Was that why it had none of its usual impact? Were they coming unhinged or already there? She met his gaze in the mirror. Her face was impassive, her voice cool.

"I'll warm up the car, if you lock up." She lifted her black, woollen overcoat and evening bag from their bed on her way out. She did not glance back at him as she spoke. She assumed he would follow.

Her four-wheel drive was parked two houses down. It looked black until she neared it, then the light thrown by the nearest street lamp revealed the rich metallic green as it gleamed in reflection off the bonnet of the vehicle. She climbed into the driver's seat and started the engine. Despite the icy evening it started first try. She let the engine hum gently as she waited for Louis. She heard his footsteps ring out loudly on the footpath, his anger echoing through the night. She looked at him approaching in the side mirror. Behind him she saw the prostitute standing at the end of the street, beneath her own carefully chosen street lamp, turn to watch him too. Could she leave St Kilda? Its bohemian chic no longer enticed her and she could certainly live without the seamier side of its nightlife. For him it was definitely home. Perhaps she had the chance to relegate her time here to an interlude.

He climbed into the car. There was little traffic as she sped along King's Way. It was a crisp winter's night and the lights of the buildings on either side shone brightly, outlining the boughs of the large, leafless trees on the nature strips in front of them. They looked interesting rather than eerie. She turned into Sturt Street and checked her watch. The trip had taken only ten minutes, something of a record. She entered the underground car park beneath the concert hall and found a parking spot.

They had not spoken a word to each other the entire trip. They climbed out of the car and walked together in a kind of robotic unison up the ramps that led into the lower echelons of the Arts Centre as they made their way to Hamer Hall. Suddenly they were met by the rich colours of the surroundings; the plush carpets and chairs, and the enthusiastic voices of the people milling around in the foyers, sipping drinks or lingering in groups by the doors to the auditorium.

She bought a programme to add to her collection and the first bell sounded. They did not wait for the announcement but made their way to their seats; the front row in the very centre of the dress circle: her father was true to form. She looked away from Louis, ignoring his presence beside her and examining the hall. People were milling in, in couples or small groups mostly. Occasionally someone walked in on their own. Typically for Melbourne in winter, black was the dominant dress code but here and there splashes of wild colour contrasted dramatically, be it in a scarf or an entire outfit. The hum of conversation in the hall surged and ebbed in waves of excited chatter, then subsided to quiet whispers as the lights fell.

The subdued lighting of the stage was plenty strong enough to make out the members of the orchestra as they filed onto it and took their seats. There was the usual shuffling, adjusting of cellos; the leader stood and the orchestra tuned at her bidding, then silence. A spotlight emerged at the edge of the stage and followed him as he walked on, with his measured yet vibrant step, all the way to the podium. There he stood directly in front of her. He bowed in acknowledgement of the loud applause that had greeted him as he came into view, building in intensity until he reached his destination. He turned, stood still for a moment, his back to the audience, his stance almost military yet somehow emphasising the elegance of his figure. His full head of hair gleamed silvery white where once it had gleamed golden. He raised his baton. Complete silence filled the hall and hung in the upstroke of his hand as it lingered in mid-air.

He brought it down and the music surged and welled, replacing the fullness of silence with the richness of sound.

She gave herself to it, immersed herself in it, let it envelop her. She felt her chest tighten, her belly ache. Her head filled with the immensity of it and slowly a kind of ease made its way into even the outer reaches of her limbs; finally her scalp began to tingle. She lost all sense of time and place, as her mind filled with images of her happiest moments, her longings, the aching pain she could just touch in glancing, even in this place. Her eyes filled with tears that spilled silently onto her cheeks and rolled unheeded down her face. Both the pain and the pleasure of it felt on the edge of what she could bear, yet she did not want the music to finish, she longed to stay in this place. She knew this was the truest way her father ever reached her; in the intense beauty of the music that he helped create. She did not know if it was the same way in which he reached the hundreds of people surrounding her at such times. She had never had the words to tell him; she knew she never would have.

The music ended and the tumultuous uproar of applause replaced it. She shifted in her seat and sat upright, as always at such times catapulted from a most private, sacred place into reality. She brushed the tears from her face almost in passing, as if in irritation. She composed her face to reflect appropriate enthusiasm. All of this happened in a moment and without any conscious thought. She joined in the applause, clapping as loudly as she could. She noticed Louis, sitting forward in his seat, clapping with great vigour, he began to cheer. Her father was bowing, gesturing to the orchestra extravagantly and to the lead violinist, shaking her hand, bowing again. He left the stage. Wave followed wave of applause. He returned and bowed again. He accepted an enormous bouquet of flowers. Finally the clapping and cheering ended. Her father left the stage and the orchestra followed. The lights came on.

People around her began to stand and leave, talking with each other in animated excitement, or with measured pleasure. She turned to Louis and reached out slowly to place her hand on his hand, where it lay on his right thigh. She squeezed it gently, feeling too the taut firmness in his thigh muscles that she loved.

"So, shall we go and see him? He's expecting us."

He met her eyes and smiled. Another gift from her father; neither of them could maintain their rage or remember their disappointment in each other after their shared pleasure; they had this moment of reprieve. He freed his hand from hers and stroked her cheek where he could see the tear stains, though she had no memory or knowledge of them.

"Yes. I want to talk to him. It's been too long."

Something in her belly tightened, but she stood silently and they made their way backstage. She knocked on his door and he swung it open.

"Anna, come in, come in, my dear."

He kissed her lightly on the cheek as she passed him and reached forward to take Louis firmly by the hand. She did not know which was greater: Louis's eagerness to embrace him, or his to do the same. In any event Louis all but bounded forward.

"Louis, it's been too long!"

"Just said the same thing to Annie!"

They were off, discussing the subtleties of the performance, how marvellous it had been. Louis had been a cellist in his teens, as well as playing the guitar. He had gone in one direction but could easily have gone in the other. He had been classically trained. "All the best rock musicians are!" How often had she heard it from both of them? She turned her back on them and looked into her father's dressing mirror. She removed her black woollen coat; Parisian and elegantly cut, another gift from him. She placed it on the chair that faced the mirror.

"It's so hot in here."

They both turned to the sound of her voice and saw her again. Her father stopped midway through whatever he had been saying to Louis.

"You look exactly like your mother, when she was young." His voice was softer; his face was filled with strange shifting emotions. "She had a dress very much like that one. I suppose you know? Must have seen it in a photograph."

"No, I didn't know." His reaction was too intense. It was more than she had anticipated, although the dress had served its purpose. She would not be discarded by him ever again in Louis's presence, not for all their language of maleness and music.

"The Shostakovich was amazing, Dad. I loved it."

"Really? What did you like about it?"

A deep red crept out over her chest, amply revealed as it was at present. Did he want to punish her for the dress? Was he truly interested and hoping she would surprise him? She floundered, muted by anxiety.

Louis came unexpectedly to her rescue. He turned to her father and looked him calmly in the eye. "It's not Anna's fault. Flick would have gutted either of the girls if they dared show any musical tendency. They're both disabled by a mother's vengeance."

Frederick Mason's eyes gleamed with mirth. Felicity had always prided herself on the determination that had eschewed the Australian passion for the abbreviation of all names. She would have hated to hear anyone refer to her in such a way, let alone a member of the family. Anna stared at Louis, not knowing whether to be grateful or angry. It was the nickname he used for her mother in private, when her mother had enraged her in some way. Now he was using it in company, with her father, without her permission. The chilling truth of his statement was overshadowed by the use of the forbidden name. Frederick too was so caught by it that the acknowledgement of a tragic loss for both him and his daughters, which Louis described so forcefully and succinctly, went almost unheeded.

A short sharp rap sounded on the dressing room door. Frederick opened it. The stage manager stood there looking flustered.

"Marvellous concert! Sorry to interrupt, but there is a message from an Adrian Hargraves for your daughter, concerning his wife Chloe Hargraves. It sounded urgent!"

"She's my daughter too! What's the message?" Frederick's concern was evident.

"He wanted Dr Mason to know that Mrs Hargraves is at the Royal Women's Hospital and that she has had an emergency operation. He specifically asked that Dr Mason turn her mobile phone on."

"Thanks, Tony. Thanks very much."

Frederick closed the door in a distracted way and turned to Anna. She looked very pale as she pulled her phone from her bag and pressed the side switch that took it off silent mode. The two men waited as she rang her message bank. She did not place the message on speaker phone and they watched her expectantly as she listened.

Anna's shoulders slumped and she grew paler still. She reached for the chair in front of her and finally sat down. She looked at her father. "Oh God. Her waters broke. She's had a cord prolapse." Tears filled her eyes. She spoke in a whisper. "Not her too."

Louis was the one to respond. "Get a grip, Anna. You need to function if you're going to play medical advocate for them. I presume that's what they want. Just ring him back, now!"

His tone carried his resentment. Chloe and her husband were no favourites of his. He felt they used Anna and that she let them. Adrian certainly only ever rang if he wanted something. This case was urgent, yet so many previous calls had been anything but. Louis was sure that it would never occur to Adrian to consider the impact a request of his might have on Anna, or on her life. It was just not in Adrian's frame of reference. Anna stiffened and sat upright. She dialled Adrian but he was not answering. She tried her mother's number too but with no success. Her mother would certainly be at the hospital. There was no way Chloe would face something like this without her.

"Anna, what exactly has happened to your sister?" Her father's voice was steady.

She looked up at him and began to speak mechanically. "She's had an emergency caesarean. She was still in recovery when Adrian left the message, but that was a few hours ago. The message was pretty muddled but it sounds like she'd been having contractions all today and they were already at the hospital when the cord prolapse happened. Maybe there's hope." She sighed deeply. "He said the baby was breach, so I guess the presenting part wasn't engaged." She looked at her father and Louis with desperation and yearning. She saw the blank expressions on both their faces.

"Translation please!" Louis's frustration and annoyance were directed at her now.

"Don't you see, her waters broke, the baby's head, or in this case its bottom, wasn't there acting like a stopper at the cervix which was dilating, so the umbilical cord fell through." She realised they had no idea of the implications of what she had just told them. She spoke very quietly but clearly, steadying her voice to make sure they heard. She knew she could not repeat it. "It means that with any contraction of the uterus the blood supply to the baby can be cut off. The baby can die or be brain damaged."

* * *

Louis drove, something he almost never did. Anna felt a sudden, unexpected sense of gratitude. Was he doing this just because he had made the effort to come to the concert sober or had he somehow, at last, fathomed her need of him? Her father had momentarily considered coming as well, then changed his mind. She had left with a promise to keep him informed. It seemed such a long way for so brief a drive; through the city at night, straight up Elizabeth Street following the empty tram tracks to Flemington Road and they would be there. This new site of the hospital was unfamiliar to her. She had done her undergraduate obstetric training and deliveries at the Royal Women's Hospital when it was a little over a kilometre away in Grattan Street. Louis pulled in at the Emergency Department entrance.

"I'm not coming in. I can't do this one." He was staring straight ahead. She wished she was in a position to say the same. She made no move to leave the car and finally he turned towards her. She looked directly in his eyes. She willed him to change his mind and come with her, so that she need not face this too on her own. He returned her stare, unmoved or unmoving, she could not fathom which. She nodded word-lessly and reached for the door.

He relented slightly. "Give me a call if you need a lift home."

"It's okay. I'll get a cab." Her voice was flat, emotionless. She climbed out and watched as he drove away.

Anna stood in in the middle of the dark driveway just outside the entrance to the Emergency Department. She felt unable to think, immobilised. She had not been anywhere near a hospital since being admitted herself, just over a year ago. It was not the same hospital, at least there was that. She realised suddenly that she was standing exactly where an ambulance would need to pull in. She stepped up onto the pavement but still could not approach the entrance doors. She tried to gather herself, to focus on what she must do. She had phoned Adrian several times but he was not answering, neither was her mother. Anna looked down at herself. There had been no time to go home or to change. She felt foolish in her formal attire, but in the end what did it matter? The outcome of what was going on at this very minute, what might already be decided, would determine the future course of her sister's life, the structure of the family, immediate and extended. A form of dress, a dress itself, was really such a trivial thing.

Large buildings loomed about her in the darkness and just ahead were the glass doors of the Emergency Department. She willed herself to move and they opened automatically as she approached them. She was surprised to find a small rectangular room, dimly lit, with a triage counter not far away and an empty waiting area to one side of it. There was no direct access to the Emergency Department, no way to sight whether it was full or empty, busy or quiet. It was an unfamiliar setup and strangely unnerving. Anna made the effort needed to function; she steeled herself and pulled her torso to its full height as she approached the triage desk. There was a serious looking woman in a hospital uniform sitting behind a glass panel staring at a computer screen. She was middle-aged, with short cropped red hair. She looked up as Anna approached her and saw the anxiety and distress in her face, but most people who arrived at this time of night were either stressed or distressed; ill, in pain, or accompanying someone who was.

Anna stood in front of the woman and fought to keep her voice calm. Her legs were trembling; she could not bear it that her voice might do the same. "My sister Chloe Hargraves has been admitted today, she's had an emergency caesarean …"

The woman cut her off, her tone efficient, her voice tired. "I'm sorry I can't help you with that." Anna's face fell and the woman continued. "All after hours maternity admissions are through there." She nodded to the doors at the far end of the room, close to where Anna had come in. "Just go through those doors and keep right, till you get to Security. They'll be able to tell you where your sister is." She turned back to the computer screen.

Anna looked across the room. She had to keep going, she was committed to this now. She crossed the room and followed a short corridor around to another set of doors that opened into the lower ground foyer of a large building. A line of grey posts connected by grey ropes cordoned her off from the foyer itself, where a large sculpture loomed beside her in the subdued light; a cluster of giant women that huddled together and gave the impression that they were on the move, heading somewhere. The symbolism eluded her. She followed the barriers that herded her to the white walls and dark glass of the security counter directly before her. The security man on duty slid the glass aside. "Can I help you?"

Anna tried again. "Good evening, I'm Dr Anna Mason. My brother-in-law rang to tell me that my sister has been admitted to the Royal Women's. She's had a caesarean." She stopped. It felt so hard to go on.

"The patient's name?" The security man was looking at her expectantly. He was thickset and friendly.

Anna realised that he wanted to help. She looked at him with gratitude. "Chloe. Chloe Hargraves."

He turned back behind the glass. She could not make out exactly what he was doing but assumed he too must be searching a computer screen. "I'm afraid your sister is not in the Royal Women's."

Anna felt a surge of dismay, followed quickly by anger with Adrian for giving her the wrong information. She fought to hide any sign of it, and even harder to keep thinking. Adrian was really frightened, he would not call her to the wrong place, but he knew nothing about hospitals and how they were run. She realised with sudden shock that she and Chloe had not discussed the specifics of her pregnancy at all, like if she was being cared for by a private obstetrician or in the public system. She could well be in the private hospital that was attached to the Women's.

"Frances Perry House. She must be there. Do you have access to their information as well?"

He could see how pent-up she was. He smiled at her kindly. "If she's there I'll find her … Yes, here she is!" He looked up at her, pleased to have been of assistance. He began speaking to her in a slow calm voice, giving her directions. He nodded towards the row of lifts facing them across the foyer. "Just take that last lift to the sixth floor of Frances Perry. It's all shut up there at this time of night. You'll have to use the intercom and someone will come out and let you know how to get to your sister."

He watched her turn away from him so tentatively, she seemed to be struggling with something. He wondered briefly about this pale, frightened woman in her evening clothes. He did not like the thought of her roving about the hospital on her own, but she said she was a doctor, surely she would be alright. The phone rang and he slid the glass window in front of him back in place before he answered it.

Anna pulled her coat around her and made sure it was fully buttoned and showed nothing of what she was wearing beneath. She hesitated a few paces from the lifts. The hospital foyer was so immense, so modern, so completely unlike the Royal Women's Hospital she had known. The space loomed about her. She studied the row of lifts and found the lift for Frances Perry House. A sudden longing to be able to ring ahead, to somehow find out what she was about to face nearly stopped her, but there was no one to ring. She moved forward and pressed the up button. As she waited for the lift to come a hard knot of anxiety began burning in her epigastrium. Her thoughts became dazed and cloudy; she struggled to think and felt suddenly dizzy.

The doors to the lift opened with their automated whooshing sound. She braced herself for some form of human interaction with whoever might come out, but the lift was empty. She walked into it, and pressed the button for the sixth floor. It was one of those rapid, lurching lifts that she had always thought so unsuitable for a hospital, for anywhere really. Her dizziness turned to nausea as her stomach heaved with the motion and the sudden stop. Then all sensation was gone as the doors opened. She stared down at the brown carpet before her, stepped onto it and lifted her gaze to the sign on a pillar directly in front of her; operating and birthing suites in one direction, she turned and headed in the other. The large plate glass windows beside her looked out over the city and the glowing lights made it seem so alive, so bright on this cold winter's night. She found the closed doors she had been told to expect and pressed the intercom.

"Dr Anna Mason, I'm here to see my sister Chloe Hargraves. She's had an emergency caesarean sometime this afternoon or evening." She was not sure how much more she had in her.

"Just a moment please." She waited for some minutes until the doors opened and a middle-aged nursing sister greeted her. "Your sister is back from theatre and in her own room on the seventh floor. I don't know if she'll be in a state for visitors as yet." Her tone was neutral, matter of fact. Handling overeager relatives was a regular part her job.

"I got a message from her husband after she was out of surgery, asking me to come. He must have left it some hours ago." Anna blushed. "I was out and only got it a little while ago. I haven't been able to contact them." Was this saying too much? Anna realised that she had lost all confidence, it felt so strange.

"I'm sure you can see her briefly at least then. I'll just come up with you. That will be easiest."

They entered the lift in silence and left it the same way. The nursing sister escorted Anna past the nurses on duty on the seventh floor, and right to the door of her sister's room. "Here we are, Dr Mason."

"I can't thank you enough." Her attempted smile of gratitude was more of a frightened grimace. The woman had already turned and was gone. Anna suddenly became aware of the smell of the hospital; that deeply familiar but subtle mix of antiseptics and bodily effusions. She realised that more than anything she wanted to turn and flee. She looked at the door in front of her, pushed it open, and walked through.

She found that she had entered another world where a nurse bent solicitously over the bed at its centre. Here a figure draped in white hospital linen lay silent and pale, pale like the moon, pale like their father, blonde hair always so bright clinging in strands around her face which was still, washed out, turned to one side on the pillow. Their mother and Adrian hovered attentively by the bedside. In this world her sister ruled supreme. She felt dizzy once more, off balance. There had been no one with her; no one, no Louis, no friend, no one to bear witness, no one to console her. The tears burnt behind her eyes, her chest tightened. Not now, she could not allow this now, not here, not with them.

She took one step, two, uncertain of her place here. Her mother looked up and saw her, such complex emotions played out in that first glance: envy, anger, hatred and somewhere relief. Was it her imagination? Could she really see all that in the instant before her mother composed her face into its habitually cool mask? The nurse turned towards her. "I'm afraid we can't have anyone else in here right now."

"Please, just for a little." It was Chloe's voice, soft, so soft, almost a whisper.

"Just a few minutes then." The nurse moved to a set of charts placed on a shelf near the window and began writing on one. She put the chart down and left the room. A few more steps and Anna was at the foot of the bed. Adrian stood at alert staring at her angrily; strangely immobilised for one so used to action, he said nothing. She gazed at Chloe who moved her head to a central position, staring back at Anna down the length of her own body, where a strange somewhat flattened bump told of the child no longer within her, the child that was missing.

Anna could not take her eyes from those of her sister. "The baby?"

Her mother was the one to answer; her tone flat and her voice devoid of any emotion. "They took him away. The paediatrician is with him. We don't know how he is."

"He …?" Anna's voice trailed off in a plaintive, hushed whisper, almost reverent in its sadness.

"This is not about you, Anna!" Her mother's voice was harsh and cruel.

She knew this dismissiveness so well, from her childhood, from her own tragedy a year ago, from last week. Had it been there all her life, even before her father left them? She could not afford the luxury of such speculation, not when she could barely control the flood of thoughts and images that threatened to engulf and overwhelm her.

All their eyes were on her. Why had she been summoned? What did they want or expect of her? If she could satisfy them, placate them, maybe she could get away from all of this. She did not look at her mother but spoke to Chloe.

"Do you want to wait till they come to tell you, or would you like me to see what I can find out?"

Adrian snorted. "For heaven's sake! Why do you think we rang you?"

She turned to him coolly. Not him, he had no right to treat her this way. He was not part of the age-old system that she grappled with. "Perhaps because I'm Chloe's sister, her only sibling?" She could hear it; she was using the superior tone that her mother was so adept at, a tone she had always hated.

"There's no need to turn on Adrian that way. They're both clearly in shock. Do you have any idea what we've all just been through?"

A blinding rage threatened to consume Anna. She fought with everything she had to hold her tongue. She looked steadily at her sister. "I was talking to Chloe, not to either of you."

A little colour had come into Chloe's face, but her eyes still looked strangely vacant and dull. She spoke quietly. "Please find out, Annie. Find out whatever you can."

It mobilised her and she turned quietly to go. She was a few steps from the bed when she looked back over her shoulder at the trio huddled in foreboding and silence.

"Oh, I forgot to tell you. Dad sent you his best. He wanted to come ..." She looked pointedly at her mother and then at Chloe. "... But he thought better of it, for your sake. I told him I'd let him know what's happening, when he can come and see you."

Chloe's eyes filled with tears and she began to sob; her words came in soft sharp gasps. "Tell him to come. Please Annie! Of course he can come."

Anna turned away in shock; away from her mother's instantaneous rage and her sister's weeping. Had Chloe ever before defied their mother's unspoken edict?

She was outside the doors before it occurred to her that she had no idea who the paediatrician she needed to speak to was, or where to find the baby. He would need a Special Care Nursery, but where would that be? The thought of approaching even one more member of hospital staff in order to find out felt impossible. She stood still. Should she call her father now? Should she call Louis? No, she had to do things one at a time. No point calling her father unless she could tell him about the baby. No point calling Louis at all. She walked out of the ward and into the foyer in front of the lifts to clear her head. She sat on a low striped seat in one corner and gazed out of the huge windows at the city lights.

"Anna? Anna Mason?"

She looked up bewildered. She had thought she was alone in the foyer. She had not heard the lift doors opening, not heard his footsteps. He seemed so normal, ordinary. Could anything or anyone be normal or ordinary now? He was tall and blond with a serious face which became far more youthful as he broke into a smile. He seemed intensely familiar. Yes, he was a memory from another time, twelve, no fifteen years ago; university, a place of so much hope and such disappointment. No "Brave New World", no escape from life's restrictions, just finding an acceptable way to live them out. She stood slowly as he approached her.

He saw recognition in her glance but also her confusion. He held his hand out to her. "Matthew Latham."

Her hand lay limp in his for a moment before she gripped it firmly and shook it. He looked at her with both curiosity and concern; her stylish coat and shoes, the elegant little black evening bag that she clutched so tightly, the pallor of her skin, and most of all, the sadness in her eyes.

"Not here on duty I suspect? Is someone you know here?"

She faltered momentarily and looked down. "Duty? Yes, perhaps duty." She lifted her head and met his eyes. Her confusion finally cleared and she found sudden clarity: it was possible he could help. "My sister's just had an emergency caesarean. I've been sent to try and find the paediatrician, to see how the baby is." She smiled awkwardly. "But I don't know who I'm looking for, or where to find them."

"The Hargraves baby?" He looked at her steadily. "I was just on my way to see the parents."

She dug her nails into the palm of her hand and tensed her calves, her feet planted firmly. "How is he?" She saw him hesitate. She had to make him tell her. "They asked me to find out. If it's bad news I'd best go back in with you. I'd like to be prepared."

"I really can't say. His Apgars were awful, meconium-stained liquor, he needed full resuscitation, but he's breathing now. He didn't need a respirator, just CPAP, which is good news as far as his lungs go. It will really be another twenty-four hours at least before we have a clearer idea about cerebral function, possibly a week for any certainty. I can't be more hopeful than that. It wouldn't be fair."

She sighed deeply. "At least he's alive."

He motioned towards the ward. "Coming with me?"

"No. I'd best ring my father first. I promised my sister I would."

He seemed strangely alert, maybe even excited. "Is he in Melbourne?"

Was that why he remembered her, because of her father? Was he another musician or classical music fanatic? "Yes, he is. I think he'd want to know as soon as possible."

"Is your mother here too?" He looked worried, concerned for her. How could that be? How well had she known him? She struggled to remember. Some phases of her younger life were such a blur. She looked at him hard. He was appealing, good looking enough. A wave of body memory caught her, deep sensual pleasure, damp sand beneath her feet, a pathway in her brain allowed her some access. Matthew! She had not thought of him for years, but how had she forgotten him?

"Anna, can I talk with you? I'll be finished in an hour. It looks like you'll be here for a while. You probably think me mad or crass, or both, given the circumstances."

She met his gaze and held it. "You can give me a lift home if you like. St Kilda? Not out of your way?"

"No. No, not at all. What about your father, won't you want to wait for him if he comes in."

"I'm not playing referee. I haven't got the stomach for it." She smiled thinly. "My parents haven't spoken to each other in years. I doubt if that will change tonight. It might all but kill my mother but I'm sure she will find some excuse to leave my sister's bedside when he comes." She looked at him intently. "Way too much information, I'm sorry."

"Don't apologise. It doesn't surprise me." His voice was hesitant, kind. "Meet me on level four, near the Intensive Care Nursery, in an hour?" She nodded assent and he headed for the ward.

She watched him as he walked away; she noted his upright stance, the squareness of his shoulders, the fact that his hair was darker at the back and had begun to go grey there. He turned in the direction of the ward and was gone. She opened her small bag and held her mobile phone in the palm of her hand. She stared at it, then turned it on and touched his number.

"Anna?"

"I hope I didn't wake you, Dad."

"Of course not! You think I could sleep. Well, tell me. The truth."

"You have a grandson. He's alive but they won't know how he's going to be for a while."

He sighed deeply. "And Chloe?"

"She's okay physically. I don't know how she's taking it. The paediatrician's just gone in to tell her. I wanted to ring you before I go back in there." She was silent for a moment, they both were. "Dad, she wants to see you. She wants you to come to the hospital."

He made a strange gasping sound. "Your mother?"

"She was there when Chloe asked me to call you."

"I've cancelled my schedule for the rest of this week. Tell Chloe I'll be there in the morning. Tell her in front of your mother. Let's see if she can meet even this with some grace or generosity!"

"I wouldn't hope for miracles, I can't recall either in my time with her." Her tone was flat. "I should go to Chloe."

"Of course, of course. Thank you, Anna. I'm sure I'll see you in there. But if we miss each other I'll call."

"Goodnight, Dad." She touched "end call" on her phone and stared at it until the screen blanked out. Her chest felt tight. Was he trying to make it up to her in some small way? He'd been in Germany a year ago, he had sent her flowers. Yet here he had cancelled a week's plans for Chloe who hardly spoke to him. She could not afford to think about it. She had to go back, had to speak to Chloe and her mother again before she left. It was the required thing and she would not be forgiven if she did less. In any case there was an hour before Matthew was going to drive her home. She remembered that he was in there with them now. She braced herself and made her way back to her sister's room.

Matthew turned to her with obvious relief and watched her as she approached the bed. "Hello Anna, I've just been filling your family in on how things stand." She gave him a small smile. "I'd best get back to the Nursery." He looked directly at Chloe. "I'll come to see you in the morning Mrs Hargraves, once I see how he's doing."

"Will I be able to see him then?" Chloe's voice was very small, her eyes beseeched him, terrified.

"Of course." He turned to include Adrian. "It would be best if you both can. He's in the Neonatal Intensive Care Nursery on the fourth floor."

Adrian nodded assent silently and looked away. Anna had never seen him at such a loss for words before, would never have thought that sympathy was a feeling she could have for him, but she had it now. Matthew nodded at her then left.

"Thank you, Annie. Thank you for finding him, for getting him to come so quickly." Chloe's voice was quivering. "At least now we know."

"What do we know? Nothing!"

They all stared at Felicity blankly. Her voice was so harsh, her rage so palpable. Anna wondered if her mother had not been spoken to, had not been heard from, when Matthew was with them. Had she been relegated to the sidelines? It might explain the vehemence of her outburst. But that assumed a logical sequence of cause and effect, something that was seldom relevant where her mother was concerned. No one said anything in response.

Instead Anna spoke to Chloe. "I can't take the credit, he found me, outside in the foyer." She stared at her sister. Her voice was soft, surprisingly kind. "He's alive Chloe, he's alive. You've got hope."

Chloe began to weep, tears streaming down her face. "Daniel, Daniel Edward Hargraves, that's his name." She looked to Adrian for confirmation and he nodded.

Anna went very pale, and she sighed deeply, audibly. Her head began to spin. Chloe looked back at her sister. "Have you rung Dad?"

"Yes …" There was no space for this; she must focus on the task at hand. "… That's why I didn't come in with Matthew." They stared at her blankly. She realised that even simple links were hard for them to make at present. "… With Dr Latham. Dad sends his love. He said he'll be here in the morning. He'd cancelled this week's schedule, even before I told him how things are for …" She hesitated, to name him was to make him real, "… Daniel."

"He's cancelled his schedule!" Their mother's voice was raucous, shrill. "And we're all supposed to be grateful for it! Chloe, I don't care if you've lost your senses with worry. It's bad enough giving your child his middle name, but that man is not to enter this hospital! I won't have it!"

The nurse attending to Chloe came into the room to check her drip at that moment and looked at them with concern. She saw Chloe lying pale and silent. "Is everything alright Chloe?"

Chloe had stopped crying but looked deeply distressed. The nurse was a kind-hearted woman with a practical nature. She hated to see a distressed mother being bullied by relatives. It was far too common. She faced Felicity Mason squarely, ready for anything that might be flung her way. "I think it best if you both leave." She turned to include Anna, though her glance towards her was conciliatory. "I have to get Chloe settled for the night. You can see her again tomorrow."

It was clear that Felicity had no intention of leaving. Anna looked from Chloe to her mother. Could she bear a taxi ride with her mother? Would she survive it? What about Matthew, would he wait expectantly for nothing? She did not have his number, nor he hers: how foolish. She could page him after dropping her mother off, leave a message. She was sure to see him again in the next few days in any case; she could explain. The thoughts raced at lightning speed in her mind; still she hesitated.

"I'll give you a lift home Felicity." It was Adrian, his voice strangely calm.

Chloe made a distressed sound. "You're leaving? I thought you'd stay with me tonight."

Adrian turned to his wife. "You need your sleep, darling. I'd best go and make some calls. Everyone will want to know. I'd just disturb you when I come back otherwise."

Anna looked at him with gratitude, Felicity with dull surprise. Adrian had never before taken charge, no matter how severe her meddling in their life.

"Mum, why don't you come with me? Adrian and Chloe need some time." She nodded at Chloe. "We'll just be outside in the foyer."

Her sister met her eyes in parting. "Annie? Pray for him? Please."

She stared back, but could not give the assent that was demanded. Not that. All the rest of this, part charade, part truth, impossible to tell where one ended, blurred, melded into the other, all of it she was prepared to go along with. But she could not agree to a direct lie, not for the sake of her sister's truth. The wall of difference that had been softening between them in this time of crisis became suddenly solid and stark in its reality once more. She turned away and beckoned to her mother.

Felicity Mason was completely unused to direct defiance, let alone a united front from her daughters. Perhaps the nurse's insistence was the clincher. Whatever the reason she accompanied her elder daughter and left the room. Outside the ward in the empty foyer the silence between them became increasingly tense as they stood before the lifts.

"Perhaps I should text Adrian and let him know we'll be downstairs. There are sure to be seats on the ground floor. You might be more comfortable there."

Her mother eyed her. "I doubt he will be long." She spoke in a clipped way, each word punctuated by the silence between it and the next. "I find it strange that my comfort is of some concern to you, when you made such a point of bringing your father into all of this."

"All of this?" Anna could feel her anger rising. Adrian would be here soon, her mother would be gone. She would make some excuse, not take the same lift, if only she could hold on till then. But something snapped inside her. "Daniel is his grandson too, just as Chloe is his child. At least that much is obvious." She turned to face her mother. "I could understand if it were me. I look so much like you that if I didn't have his hands, I might doubt he were my father, yet you allow me my relationship with him. But Chloe is a female version of him. Is that why you have worked so hard to keep her from him? To deny him the pleasure he might have because she is so like him?"

"Pah, you were always his favourite and he yours! Do you think I would let another child turn to him, when he had already begun to turn away from me?"

She saw her mother's hatred and bitterness so clearly, it was so familiar, so much a part of what seemed like every waking, breathing moment of the life she had spent in her mother's presence. No, there was no past tense about it. It was here with them now, it shaped their existence together, formed the matrix in which they could relate, bound them to the limitations of its meanness. Had there been more to her mother once? What had her father found to love, the loss of which seemed to cripple him from ever risking true intimacy again? Was it fair to lay that at her mother's door or was it something her parents shared in different forms, something that might have led them to each other to live out just this tragedy. Most of all she feared it in herself, the voice, so like her mother's, which had turned with such vehemence on Louis in the past year. How could their relationship possibly hope to survive it?

"Chloe is three years younger than you, Anna, and Adrian is far younger than Louis. They have a stable life, a real chance at a family. Don't cause this mayhem in their lives."

"What?" Anna felt her head begin to spin and fought against the murky pressure not to think that had begun to take hold. She must use her rational mind, mount an argument, it was the only way out. "I'm hardly past it! Anyway 'the mayhem', as you call it, is not about Dad visiting, or not as far as anyone else is concerned. It's about whether Daniel will live or have a chance at a normal life." She realised suddenly that her mother had not said one word about Daniel, had not as far as she knew asked a single question of Matthew, had shown no desire to see the baby boy herself. Anna did not begin to understand why, but it brought her some relief regarding her mother's complete lack of any concern or compassion in her own case. There was simply something missing in her.

* * *

"If I hear one more word on the subject, Felicity Callahan, you'll be forgetting your supper as well this evening." Sister Agnes raised her eyebrows and spoke with her calm voice, the one that brooked no defiance.

Felicity was one of her most able students and quite unused to the punishments meted out to her classmates. Her face went red with rage and humiliation, to the very roots of her dark hair, but she made her way silently to the far corner of the room to stand as directed with her back to the class. She could not abide being hungry and she was to miss lunch. No one sniggered as they might have had it been Martha Kelly sent to the same corner for the umpteenth time. Felicity's rigid back, her head held high even in disgrace, defied any member of the class to dare her wrath. She intimidated them all with her beauty and her intelligence, but most of all with her aloofness and superiority and the sharp and cruel things that came unbidden from her tongue.

She stood in silence, oblivious to the lesson going on behind her. Her respect for anything that Sister Agnes might say or try to teach her in the future plummeted, caved in by the force of her outrage. If she was to be shamed for raising Darwin's name in argument, then this whole dogma must be flawed. She would never forgive Sister Agnes and would never again ask an honest question of her or of any other nun in this school. She would abide by their doctrines and find some way to pursue her own interests and beliefs as she could. There was a very good library in the township of Ballarat and at weekends they were able to go there to read. Any books they might borrow were checked on their return to the school, but that could be negotiated somehow. She stared at a small circle on the wall directly to the right of her; the green paint there was chipped and peeling. She suddenly had no stomach for this run-down school with its limited outlook.

There were five more weeks to be borne until end of term and holidays and what hope then? She would be expected to work tirelessly from the moment she returned to the farm until they sent her back here again. To work for what, a farm that she had been told most directly was her brother Jonathan's future, not hers. However inadequate this school, it was her only option for a different life. She must endure it and work to get herself to teachers' college or perhaps even to university if she could get a scholarship. She had to find her way into another world than the one she currently inhabited if she was to survive and not go mad or fade away like her mother. For now, she held tight to a hard and bitter place inside her, a place that gave her the strength to go on.

They had sent her here at the age of nine when her baby brother Andrew died suddenly of diphtheria. Her mother had lost her mind then, or so it seemed, for she spent the weeks after Andrew's death simply crying, unable to function. However, by the time Felicity returned home that Christmas it was far worse: her mother was only an empty shadow of the mother she had known before; a brittle being going through the motions of life on the farm with no substance to her and certainly no mind for her daughter. Seven years later Felicity had long forgotten her yearning to find the home and mother she had once known when she returned to the farm, or her rage at Andrew, a baby she had truly loved, for being born to wreak this havoc in her life and the life of her family.

The bell rang loudly and Felicity walked silently back to her desk to pick up her books. She looked at no one and no one attempted to catch her eye. She waited until about half the class had filed out of the room before she joined the stream heading for the corridor. Once there they all began making for the dining room, a noisy chatter emanating from the throng in happy anticipation of a hot lunch. It was icy cold and she pulled the sleeves of her grey jumper down over her hands as she cradled her books to her chest and moved against the flow. She was going to the dormitory instead.

"Felicity, what are you doing? What about lunch?" It was Amy Magill, her room-mate. Amy was relatively new here and one of the very few girls in this place or anywhere that she had ever considered a friend. "Felicity, wait!"

Felicity could not bear the indignity of telling Amy what had happened. No doubt she would hear about it from someone else soon enough. They would all be secretly pleased that this had happened to her, she was sure of it. Maybe even Amy?

But no, Amy was not like the others. She had never heard her say an unkind thing about anyone. It was in truth a strange thing that they should be friends, for most of her own thoughts about the girls around them were very unkind; she saw little to admire in any of them, though in the main she kept this to herself.

Amy had forced her way through the mass of girls and tugged at Felicity's sleeve. "Hold on, Felicity. What's the matter?"

"What makes you think anything's the matter?" Felicity's anger surged at the very thought of what had happened.

Amy looked at her incredulously. "And when have you ever missed lunch? Are you feeling sick?"

Sympathy was something Felicity could not abide. She looked Amy up and down in a cool superior way and focused her gaze on Amy's plump midriff as she spoke. "Not everyone is as desperate for food or as greedy as you are, Amy. I have work to do. I can wait till dinner."

Amy's round good-natured face fell and she blushed deeply. She did not understand what had just happened, and turned aside wordlessly to hide her unexpected tears. Felicity walked away. She realised that she felt a little better, lighter somehow; the sting and indignity of what had happened to her seemed less.

* * *

They heard his footsteps behind them and turned to greet Adrian. He was a tall, slender man, with short, brown hair and a proper air that usually never left him. His one striking feature, a pair of intense blue eyes, was safely hidden behind heavy, dark-rimmed glasses. Right now he looked wan and exhausted, closer to human than Anna had ever seen him.

"Thank you for your generous hospitality, Felicity. We were so lucky to be staying with you today. I hate to think what might have happened if we'd been in Ballarat."

Her mother beamed, her place restored, confidence revived. "You know it's my pleasure, Adrian. There's nothing I wouldn't do for you and Chloe."

Anna looked at him with renewed dislike, and her sympathy for him evaporated. Had his apparent moment of fortitude been nothing more than a wimpy, self-serving ploy? Yet perhaps he was right: if Chloe had decided to see an obstetrician in Melbourne just to be near their mother it may ironically have saved her son. Their mother hated Ballarat.

Adrian pushed the button for the lift and it came almost immediately. He and her mother entered it, and looked at her in surprise when she did not.

"I've just got something to attend to."

Adrian spoke to her flatly. "Don't go back in there and upset Chloe."

She gave him a look of disgust as the lift doors closed, preventing anything else that might have passed between them. She really had nothing to do on this floor. She just could not bear standing that close to both of them in a confined space, let alone the pretence of leaving the hospital that might follow. She had had enough of charades.

Anna waited for some time, until she could be sure that her mother and Adrian would not suddenly return for something they had forgotten, then she summoned the lift. What floor had Matthew wanted her to meet him on? She struggled to remember then pressed the button for the fourth floor. Why did he want her to meet him on the fourth floor? The Intensive Care Nursery, he had asked her to wait near there. Would she embarrass him if she asked to be admitted? Would she be breaching hospital policy? She felt a desperate urge to go there even though she recognised that she had no right to see Daniel before his parents did, and she knew she ought not to go in any case, for her own sake. It would not be wise for her. She had coped thus far: why test it? She had found it so difficult at first last year but eventually she had been able to treat babies at work, even neonates—no, newborns—it was better to call them newborns. Medical terms seemed designed to alienate one from the human side of life. A newborn was someone's precious baby, the newest member of a family, the source of such wonder and hope and fear. A neonate was a statistic, destined to survive and thrive, or not.

Once on the fourth floor she followed the signs to the Neonatal Intensive Care Unit and was surprised to find a waiting area with large bright red chairs to one side of an empty reception counter, ahead of which were the closed doors to the unit. An intercom hung on the wall just outside. She almost touched it but stopped, imagining the scene; the humidicribs, the tubing, the ventilators, the nurses or doctors attending to their tiny patients under bright or subdued lights. She felt woozy and off balance. Nausea surged in her. What folly to even consider it. She turned and headed back to the lifts. She wished she had said no to Matthew. She could still head down to the ground floor and call for a taxi. He would understand. There was a door to the stairwell beside the lift. She began to open it but had a sudden vivid image of herself tripping in her stilettos and lying at the base of the stairs in a crushed and crumpled, lifeless ball. She remembered the waiting area, the comfortable chairs. Matthew had been thinking of her. She would wait. She walked back and lowered herself into the closest chair and placed her small bag on her lap. She laid her arms on those of the chair. She leaned back and rested, for the first time in how many days or was it really weeks or even months?

* * *

The sun beamed in through the large windows. Anna sat on the bed and stared past the pale blue curtains at the city buildings bathed in the deep golden rays of autumn light, but she could not see the sharply defined detail; the rich reds and browns of brickwork, the contrasting deep greys of bluestone.

All she saw were blocks of shape and colour. She could not focus. She dared not think. She got off the bed and paced back and forth in front of the windows. This couldn't be happening. Everything ached, but most of all her engorged breasts. She grabbed her mobile phone and rang Louis's number for the tenth or fifteenth time in as many minutes. "This service is not responding …" She ended the call before the message was complete. California was seventeen hours behind at this time of year. She had sent urgent texts. How could he possibly have his phone off for so long?

She collapsed on the side of the bed, drew her legs onto it, and curled up in a foetal position. Her body began to shake and she began to sob silently. She was caught in some compulsive loop. She could not get past her urgent need to talk to Louis, to let him know. He'd come straight home, she was sure of it. She couldn't do this alone. Five weeks early, meconium-stained liquor, so unexpected, everything had been going so well, such an easy pregnancy; Infant Respiratory Distress Syndrome: he might die. They said he might die. How could it have happened? Strange early contractions, she'd come in to be monitored, foetal distress, induction, wrenching contractions she could barely remember, all her will focused on the hope that he would be born, survive. She hadn't even held him. He'd been whisked away from her, she'd heard him being suctioned, resuscitated. She knew he was intubated and on respiratory support.

She needed to get dressed and go to him. How could she go to him without reaching Louis, without letting him know that their son was born? There was no one here, no one. Chloe and Adrian were overseas. She couldn't ring her mother. Louis and her mother hated each other. She couldn't let her mother know before Louis, he would never forgive her. Her agitation began to spiral into panic. Her heart was racing and she felt like she might vomit. The door opened and the midwife who had been to see her earlier walked in. She was a caring woman. She stood by the bed and held Anna gently by the shoulder.

"It might help if you sit up." She reached forward and offered her other hand to Anna, helping her sit upright and swivel towards the end of the bed.

"Still no luck reaching your boyfriend?"

Anna winced; it was not a term she could ever use for Louis. She may not have married him, but he was so much more.

The nurse was perceptive, apologetic. "I mean your partner, your baby's father."

"No, no luck."

"Why don't I get your dressing gown and we can wander down to the Intensive Care Nursery? You should be there, if you can bear to be."

"Yes, yes I have to go there. Can you give me a moment please, I want to dress first."

She stood beside the humidicrib. She could not remember getting there; she had let the midwife lead her. She had forgotten this kind woman's name. She didn't know how to ask it again. She gazed at him, his full head of dark hair, his arms and legs that seemed long for his body, just like Louis's, but splayed at angles, a drip bandaged into one arm. His eyes were closed. His face was distorted by the tube in his mouth attached to the ventilator. His chest moved in and out in time to the strange mechanised sound of the machine. She fought to block it out. She gazed at his face. He was so beautiful.

"You can put your hand through here." The midwife put her own hand through the porthole in the humidicrib. She touched him.

Anna put her hand through, and stroked his arm. She moved her hand and gently, so very gently stroked his hair. She let her hand rest tenderly by his head. He did not respond in any way but she hoped that he sensed her.

"I'm here, darling, I'm here."

The paediatrician saw her and moved towards her with a solemn face. "Anna Mason? Hi, I'm Debra Phillips. I'm afraid the news is not good."

Anna steeled herself. Whatever happened she was not going to leave him.

* * *

Her sister had a son and he was alive. That fact sat like an object in her mind, in her being. There was so much uncertainty in his small life that it was strange that it brought her this sense of relief, strange and unexpected, but welcome. She realised that she longed for this baby to survive, to be well, to have a normal chance at life. She had feared that she would not be able to do any of these things, that she would so envy Chloe her baby that she might not be able to care for it at all. Yet here he was, a boy at that, and something in her almost wished she could pray, momentarily longed for the respite and hope permitted those who lived with that kind of belief or faith.

Neither of her parents had been religious and she had been raised an atheist. Chloe had found religion of her own accord; it came along with Adrian and she had embraced both with fervour. Her move to Ballarat to be near his family had put far less distance between them than Chloe's sudden conversion to Christianity and the Anglican Church. More precisely it was the conservatism and propriety and the strange superiority and condescension that came with Chloe's way of being a Christian that made Anna often feel like she no longer knew her sister at all. Yet, in this moment of crisis, faced with such aching uncertainty, she at last glimpsed something she could understand in her sister's new way of life. Suddenly her mind opened to Chloe and she saw the bland certainty in her life with Adrian, with his parents, as teachers in the same school, within the church community they were so involved in.

There was a structure and meaning to it all that might actually be life-saving for Chloe, who had come so close to the edge on more than one occasion in her teens. In truth, if she could conjure up a deity, or appeal to some sense of meaning in the universe, she would put in a plea for a normal life for this tiny boy, or at least a normal brain with which to negotiate the life his parents would foist on him and the reasoning capacity to make his own decisions. But that was not her understanding of how religions worked. She must surely offer something, some pledge or penance in return. She stopped abruptly. Her mind went blank.

A nurse walked by and looked at Anna as she passed. She had her head back, resting on the chair, and her eyes closed. The nurse was about to enter the Neonatal Intensive Care Unit but stopped, turned around and walked back to Anna. She was in her late twenties, a petite young woman with a serious face and thick brown hair pulled back in a ponytail. Anna did not hear the footsteps, so deep was she in her own thoughts or so removed from them, but she suddenly felt the other woman's presence near her. She opened her eyes and looked up into the nurse's face.

"Are you all right? Are you here to visit someone?" There was genuine concern in the voice.

"I'm fine thank you. I've just seen my sister in Frances Perry House. I'm waiting for my lift home."

The nurse stared at her hard. A look of annoyance came into her face as she noticed Anna's coat and evening bag. Anna saw the change and spoke at once, her tone placating. "Dr Latham is treating my nephew. He's an old friend. He offered to take me home and asked me to wait here."

The nurse blushed immediately. She looked away and back again. She hesitated before she spoke. "I'm sure that will be fine then." Her voice was soft, almost sad. She took a step towards the closed doors then turned back to Anna. "What's your name?"

Anna looked at her with surprise. She was sure that she did not look dangerous or like someone about to cause any sort of trouble. "Anna Mason. Dr Anna Mason."

The colour in the younger woman's cheeks and on her neck deepened. "Right, okay." She stood staring at Anna in a strange way, then turned, the doors opened and she walked ahead.

Anna closed her eyes again. She was not wearing a watch and had lost all sense of time, but she somehow knew that Matthew would come when he had said he would or there would be a good reason if he did not, that he would find her eventually and take her home. Home, home and Louis, her chest tightened and she swallowed hard with sadness. She pulled her thoughts away to work, how many hours before she had to be there? How could she find it in her to function as she needed to? She somehow always did. A sudden thought unsettled her; if her father could take the week off, why couldn't she? If he was going to be in Melbourne and visiting Chloe in hospital, if her parents might be in the same building or even the same room for the first time in twenty something years, why couldn't she be here as well?

She heard footsteps. She opened her eyes and saw Matthew standing directly in front of her. He looked at her gravely, then smiled, held out his hand, and helped her to her feet. "You look absolutely bushed. Come on, let's get you home."

She let him lead her to the lift and to the hospital car park. They walked beside each other with such ease. Anna felt an unexpected sense of comfort. It was a relief to rely on someone, to know that he would get her home safely, that she need not be vigilant, albeit for half an hour or maybe less. It did not occur to her to question why she trusted him so implicitly.

She closed her eyes and listened to the hum of the engine as the car started and slowly began to move. She heard him rustling about, touching switches, turning dials. She felt a blast of air that began to have some warmth in it.

"Could you turn it off please? I need the cold right now, to clear my head."

He adjusted something and the air soon had a bite to it. She smiled and turned her head slowly in his direction, then opened her eyes. He loomed so close, yet still felt strangely comforting sitting there, earnestly focused on the road as they made their way from the hospital into the crisp, dark night and the empty roads snaking their way back to her house.

He turned to look at her, a brief glimpse to check that she was really there. She met his eyes for an instant before he turned back to the road. "So, Matthew Latham, I know that you're a paediatrician now, but precious little else about what's happened in your life. Still, here I am in your car."

"Not for the first time, Anna."

She ignored his statement. "Are you married?"

"Technically, yes. My divorce is about to come through, but I've been separated for two years. I have a little girl, Rose, she's five." He turned to look at her again, to see if she was listening. She was sitting up and staring at him. "She's at kinder, well pre-prep, starts school properly next year, but it's at the same place. This year was the big one for her, starting there."

He looked ahead once more but spoke with more confidence. "It's so hard not being with her. I see her every second week-end and one night each week. I'm hoping when she's older it will be more. It makes my work hard; I'm always with other children, not with her. I would have stayed longer in the rela-tionship, even though it wasn't working, just to have time with her. But her mother found someone else." He stopped short. "I'm sorry. You got a lot more than you asked for." It had just poured out of him. His tone softened again. "Do you have any children, Anna?"

"I had a son, Anton, but he died." Her voice faltered, her eyes filled with tears, she was determined to say it and loudly enough that he could hear. Someone had to hear. "He died when he was only one day old."

"I'm so sorry." He sounded deeply touched, sincere.

It gave her courage to go on. "But the hardest thing you see is that everyone acts as though he never existed, as if he wasn't real." Her face twisted into a mask of pain. She looked at him and the tears spilled from her eyes. "It makes me feel like I'm quite crazy at times."

His face was full of sorrow but he did not turn to look at her, his eyes were fixed on the road ahead. He spoke slowly. "Was he Louis Williams's son?"

She sat up further, surprised and on alert. "Yes."

"I've seen you together a few times over the years; in Chapel Street at a café, at Elwood beach. I was right next to you in a bookshop in Acland Street one time some years ago. I almost said hello."

She sighed. "I guess it's part of being with someone famous, you always get noticed." She thought of Louis, thought of her father, of her life with each of them. "At times I long for anonymity."

He laughed strangely. "I didn't see you because you were with him, Anna. I saw you, then I noticed him."

She struggled with her disbelief. "Really?"

"You don't remember do you?" His voice held a kind of confused acceptance at the irony of life.

"Only a little. Tell me."

He spoke slowly, his words measured. "You changed my life, Anna Mason. You saved me, gave me hope when I needed it. We spent an amazing weekend at Flinders in my aunt's holiday house. It was two weeks after my mother died of lymphoma. We told each other everything. We made love everywhere, all weekend. You were, still are, the warmest thing I've ever known. I knew we couldn't be together. I was too sad. I wasn't good for you. But I've been looking for someone like you ever since."

* * *

He had gone back to the house to get her a jacket. She stood by the water's edge and watched him getting bigger and bigger as he returned; clambering over the dunes and making his way laboriously across the stretch of soft sand between them.

His blond hair was wild in the wind, whipping across his face, into his eyes. He fought with it to see where he was going. He was so beautiful, so kind. She turned back to face the sea and stood barefoot, gripping the firm, wet sand with her toes. An icy wave lapped over her feet and they went numb. She clutched her runners absent-mindedly in her right hand.

"Annie, what are you doing? You're blue with cold!"

He moved her up the beach away from the water's edge and wrapped her in the large coat he had brought with him; dressing her like a baby, threading her arms into the sleeves, tying the belt around her waist. He took her shoes from her hand and placed them on the sand. She stood facing him. He was much taller than her. She was not used to looking up at anyone.

"You're shivering. Here." He took her hands in his and began to rub them.

She pulled her hands free and flung her arms around him. She hugged him fiercely, desperately willing his closeness to give her the something that was missing. This was all wrong, she should be comforting him. It was his mother who had died two weeks ago. Chloe was in hospital, but she was alive.

She bent and picked up her shoes. "Come, let's walk, I need to walk."

He wrapped his arm around her shoulders, she hugged his waist, her other hand reaching up, lacing her fingers through his hand that hung from her shoulder. She loved the firmness of his body, the tenderness of his touch. She had never known anyone like him; so passionate, so gentle, so easy to be with. They had somehow avoided this for the two and a half years they had spent together at university. They were alphabetically aligned, fated to meet in tutorials and prac groups. They had hovered in each other's orbit, acknowledging each other but keeping their distance among the 200 in their year level that moved as a swarm through the sandstone cloisters and across the grassy courtyards; from the science blocks to the medical school of Melbourne University.

They walked in silence, buffeted by the wind, each caught in their own turmoil or sorrow, comforted by the presence of the other. The beach was strangely empty, theirs, a midwinter's gift when they needed it. He stopped suddenly and stood silent. She looked up at him. "What is it? Tell me."

"I just wish we'd done this long ago. I wish you'd got to know her. She would have loved you, been so pleased for me." His eyes filled with tears and he began to sob quietly. His body shook. She didn't know what to do. She had never seen a man cry before. No one in her family cried except Chloe, who raged and wept and played her strange game of life and death at everyone else's expense. This was so different. She found it hard to consider what he had lost; a mother he loved and depended on who wished him well. What would that feel like?

They turned and fought the wind all the way back to the house. They hurried over the threshold suddenly eager for the warmth within. He stoked the fire in the pot-bellied stove and it soon heated the small lounge room. It was dusk and she rose from the deep couch where she had sat to watch him at work. She moved to the windows and began to close the curtains: strange, still bright bunches of red waratah on faded brown poplin. He came up behind her and ran his fingers through her hair, traced a line from the nape of her neck to the small of her back, then up between her shoulder blades. She leant into him, loving his hardness and his hands that roved freely over her. She turned and lost herself in his kiss. He pulled her back to the fire.

She half raised herself on her outstretched arm and looked down at his face as he lay beside her naked, spent, replete.

"What would your aunt think if she knew we were here like this?"

He smiled, not opening his eyes. "I'm sure we're not the first." He laughed. "What a strange thought!"

"Maybe I am strange."

He still did not open his eyes. "That's not what I said."

"But perhaps it's true."

"You know my aunt might actually be glad for me, that I can find some happiness at a time like this … Why do you think you're strange?"

Her face became sombre, solemn. She did not speak. He opened his eyes and looked up at her. He reached up and stroked her face. She looked down at him. "If I told you, I think it might be very hard for you to like me."

"Annie, you're crazy! You're gorgeous. I know all that stuff about your family has been hard to tell. But whatever your mother or your sister have done, has to do with them, not you. Christ, what a nightmare finding your sister like that. She's so bloody lucky you came home when you did and called the ambulance." He turned her face so that he could look directly into her eyes. "You saved her life, Anna."

"Maybe, but the awful thing is, at times I wish I hadn't got home in time." She closed her eyes and turned her head away.

* * *

Shadowy images entered her mind as he spoke. They began to have colour and hue, but would shimmer or fracture then vanish before they could fully take form. Yet she knew he was speaking the truth. She had a sudden desire to be absolutely honest with him. "I'm sorry Mathew. All I have is a sense of you and these patchy memories. I guess it says a lot about my life back then, I was really messed up in a lot of ways." Was it a true statement? She had smoked a bit too much marijuana, drunk a bit too much wine, but never to a state of oblivion, surely? Was it around the time of one of Chloe's suicide attempts? It was the right era. Those times had holes in them all over the place. Trying to remember what actually happened was like trawling through mud. Or was it that the intimacy he spoke of was far more than she had a capacity to sustain, then or maybe even now?

"Doesn't do a great deal for my ego but I appreciate you being direct. Well, here we are." The car pulled into the curb and he turned off the engine. "Are you still with him, Anna?" He sounded concerned, almost disapproving.

She unbuckled her seat belt and swivelled in her seat to face him. She raised an eyebrow. "A weekend together in our late teens means you get to question my life choices?"

"I have no right." His voice was soothing. "Forgive me, please?"

She softened. "Thanks for the lift." She remembered that he had listened, truly listened about Anton. "I'm sure I'll see you in at the Women's over the next few days." She reached out and took his hand. She grasped it firmly. "I'm sorry if I'm not who you expected to find."

"You're so much more!" He saw the incredulity and pain in her face. "Really!"

She stared at him for a moment before she spoke. "By the way, there was a nurse on the fourth floor who asked me what I was doing there. She got very flustered when I mentioned you were driving me home, brown hair, serious face, pretty. I hope I haven't caused any trouble."

He laughed out loud. "Hardly! I'm the one who asked you to wait there. Sue Evans means nothing to me. We aren't seeing each other."

She looked at him archly. "But you know you mean something to her?"

"Goodnight, Anna."

"Goodnight, Matthew. I'll see you soon." She climbed from the car and walked through her front gate and onto the porch.

Louis had not left the outside light on and she fumbled in the dark for her keys, then remembered that he had taken them to drive home. She heard Matthew drive away as she reached for the bell, but the door swung open before she could press it. Louis stood in front of her, hands on hips and seething.

"So who was the guy in the Merc?"

"What? Oh, he's the paediatrician looking after Chloe's son. We were in the same year at university. He was kind enough to drive me home."

"Kind enough." His tone was nasty, mocking. "You both looked very cosy out there, chattering away like little birds." He was making his hands talk to each other like puppets right in front of her face.

She could smell the alcohol on his breath. She looked at him with disgust. "This is life and death stuff, Louis. You haven't asked about the baby at all, or about Chloe. What's happened to you? I'm exhausted. I'm going to sleep in the spare room." She tried to push past him.

"Oh no you don't, Anna. No you don't!" He put his arm around her waist and pulled her body forcefully against his. "You talk to me like I have no feeling, like I'm some sort of robot you share a house with."

She tried to push away from him but he held her tighter. "Have you any feelings, really? About anything that counts?" She heard her voice and how high-pitched and strange it sounded. She began to sob, great wrenching sobs that welled up from inside her. Her body shook with them.

He held her tighter, clung to her. He too began to cry, but softly, silently. He ran his hands over her hair, then her body. "Shush, baby, shush. It's okay, sweet Annie. It's okay." Slowly she began to relax against him. She felt her body meld into his. It was so familiar and so compelling. She still loved the feel of his touch. She knew she always would; the urgency and the tenderness of it. Whatever his mood, whatever his mouth might say, his body was always like this, loving and urgent. As if there was nothing else in the world in that moment but she and he and this thing that pulsed between them, this need to lose themselves in each other. She wished she could hold her resolve and push him away, walk down the corridor and into the spare room, bolt the door behind her. But there was no bolt in any case and her body longed for his. She tilted her head and raised her mouth to his. She hated the acrid smell of alcohol on his breath but she closed her mind to it, shut it out.

He pushed her against the wall and started to remove her coat. She grabbed his hand and led him to their bedroom. He was undressing her but fumbling as he went. She moved slightly away from him and began to undress herself. He did the same and seemed to make a better job of it. Once naked she suddenly felt how cold the house was. He had not turned the heating on. She began to shiver. She turned the bedside light on and the harsh glare of the overhead light off and rushed into bed to huddle beneath the cover of the doona. She watched him as he walked towards the bed. He still had his erection but her passion was waning. A wave of enormous sadness began to engulf her. He climbed into bed beside her and reached for her. She pushed the sadness away and touched him in response. She did not know how many times this would happen again between them, but she wanted it now. She needed it this night.

FOUR

She woke and felt strangely confused and disorientated. The room was still dark and the world quite silent. She glanced across to the bedside table and the illuminated dial on the clock radio. Seven a.m. She had forgotten to set the alarm but something had woken her. Louis lay cuddling a pillow, sprawled out and deeply asleep beside her. She was not late for work, so why the strange sense of urgency. She was sure there was something she needed to do. Then she remembered. She felt anxious at the thought of it all. She sat up slowly and climbed out of bed, cautious not to wake him. She stepped over the pile of clothes on the floor and pulled her woollen dressing gown from the back of the bedroom door. She bent over and rummaged among the pile of shoes, almost all Louis's, under the dressing table till she found her winter slippers. She slid them on and walked out of the room closing the door firmly behind her. She picked up her little evening bag from the hall table, switched the central heating on and made her way to the kitchen.

She shut the kitchen door quietly and sank onto the nearest chair by the table. "Bugger him!" Two empty bottles, a half-filled glass and spilled wine dried in rings just where she had placed her bag on the table; it was made of Huon pine and one of the few things that she treasured, but why would that count?

Enough, she had to stop it, this didn't matter. She opened her bag and reached into it for her phone. She switched it on and checked for messages, then sat staring at it. She picked it up and dialled. "Bill? Hi, it's Anna. Sorry to ring so early. I had to catch you before work." Her hand was trembling. "I can't make it today. In fact I need to take the whole week off. Chloe's had her baby. It was an undiagnosed breach with a cord prolapse. She had a caesar. He's in Neonatal Intensive Care, they're not sure of his prognosis." She choked on the words but hurried on. "My Dad's in town and staying on. I need to be there."

"I'm so sorry to hear about Chloe, but it's about time, Anna. Of course you should take the week off, take two weeks if you need to. You should have done this months ago."

She realised he had been hinting at it for a long time. He was the reason she had joined the clinic really, and the reason she stayed. The ten years between them made him seem fatherly. No, it was his concern for her that was evident but never foisted on her that did it. They went about their work, rarely spoke beyond daily greetings and pleasantries or the discussion of work issues and patient care, socialised at Christmas time and had a deep respect for each other's practice of medicine.

"I'll let Don know he'll be a lot busier this week." He laughed. She realised suddenly that they both carried Don. It was not just her, though it often felt that way.

"Why don't we talk on the weekend? See how things stand by then."

"I can't thank you enough, Bill."

Easy, after all, just that easy. She had been so driven, unable to stop working, needing to feel needed. Yet she could simply stop. Could she stop the other too; stop calculating when she might be most fertile, making a fool of herself by trying to drag Louis somewhere he dreaded, hating him for rejecting her? Her head began to ache and she felt muddled again, oppressed. She looked at the damaged table, felt her anger rising, and her head begin to clear. It was not just her doing, he had his part. She could no longer take responsibility for all of it.

The door opened and Louis stood in the doorway. He looked at her in surprise as she sat at the table deep in thought. He took the few steps to reach her and brushed her cheek lightly with his fingers. "What, babe, not going to work today?"

"No, I'm going to the hospital to be with Chloe. Dad's staying in Melbourne. He's cancelled his engagements and taken the week off. I figured if he could do it, so could I. So I've just cleared it with Bill." She paused. "Come with me?" She looked at him intently waiting for his reaction.

"You don't get it, do you? No hospitals. No babies." He walked to the sink and spat in it, then rinsed his mouth. "How will Zig and Zag manage without their best girl? I thought you were indispensable?"

She studied his back with loathing. He turned suddenly and stared at her strangely, the hand on each side of his body gripping the bench fiercely, turning white at the knuckles, trembling slightly. She looked down, rubbed her finger on the nearest wine stain, then looked up at him, her face disdainful, her eyebrow arched.

"I can read your mind." His words were soft, stilted. "I know exactly what you're thinking; just how kind and understanding Bill is, not some uncouth drunken excuse for a man who's ruined your precious table and your life." He glared at her. "Tell me I'm wrong."

She started slightly in surprise but said nothing.

"If Bill's so magnanimous and considerate why didn't he insist you slow down, tell you to stop when it might have done some good!" He was shouting. "They feel sorry for you, you know, that pair of clowns! Sorry for you because you're with me, because you haven't settled for their suburban dream." He stopped, attempting to settle himself, then spoke again, his tone pleading. "Do you know how it feels to be that man,

Anna? I don't give a fuck what they think, but to be that man to you?"

Her voice was icy. "What do you mean, when it could have done some good?"

He stared at her and faltered for a moment, averting his eyes. She felt her stomach griping, a pit of nausea and pain. She stood abruptly. "You know what? I don't care! I can't do this right now, there's too much at stake. Chloe had a boy, Daniel." She drove the words at him, wanted them to hurt: he had to hear. He was not going to avoid it all this time. "They don't know if he'll live or be okay. I need to get to the hospital."

"There's nothing at stake for you there, honey. That's Chloe's baby, not yours."

* * *

Eight a.m. She pulled her black woollen coat about her and hid the lower part of her face in her scarf as she joined a small group of workers waiting for a tram to take them into the city. Eight a.m. on a winter's morning in Melbourne with the world going to work. If she caught the tram now she would turn up at the hospital far too early. She could not go back to the house and Louis. Her long skirt flared around her legs meeting her boots at mid-calf. She was dressed for comfort, could stay out all day, but where was she to go? A strange sense of unreality was with her, one that was familiar, that came at times of personal crisis. Dealing with crises in the lives of patients was far simpler; she could usually sort out rapidly if and how she could be of help, where to find additional assistance as needed: it was enabling. Set adrift without the structure of her ordinary routine, the day stretched before her with numbing uncertainty.

She detached herself from the group of would-be passengers and began to walk. She stopped at the takeaway window of the first in a string of cafés. She ordered coffee and a croissant from the chatty waiter. She noted his gleaming ear stud,

66

his nose ring, hair gelled in an upward wave and tight-fitting, black shirt blazoned with red writing. She clutched the brown paper bag in her left hand and held the cardboard cup with its plastic lid firmly in her right. She began to stride out, her steps giving her purpose, down Acland Street into Fitzroy Street. She bypassed the light-rail and headed out across the ovals that led to Albert Park Lake. There were others walking, but not many. The wind had a bite to it and the sky was dull grey. She sat on a bench fifty metres from the lake and opened her paper bag. The croissant was rich, buttery, and still surprisingly warm. The sip of coffee from its insulated cup burnt her lip and made her start; she pulled backwards to avoid spilling it. She sipped at the cup more cautiously. She drained the strong soothing liquid slowly as she watched the surface of the lake get whipped into little caps by the wind.

She reached into her handbag and pulled out her phone. How many years had passed since she'd felt she had a legitimate reason to call her father two days in a row, that she wouldn't be disturbing him, or interrupting his schedule? But what would she say to him? She couldn't tell him that she had the week off, that she'd followed his lead, that she wanted to be part of whatever was about to unfold. She feared he too would tell her it had nothing to do with her, that this was not her baby. "Stay away, Anna, let your mother and I fight over your sister". She could not bear even the fantasy of it. She put the phone away. She stood and began to walk again. Her body had felt so useless for so long, such a failure. She needed to walk.

How far would it be; four, six, eight kilometres? Her sense of distance had never been good. It didn't matter. Time, for once she had time. She walked by the lake shore, so sterile now, the big gum trees of her childhood gone for the sake of a racetrack once a year. No little yachts flying across blue waters as on a summer's day; just grey dancing peaks before the wind. She pulled the scarf away from her face and felt the chill of the air; the sting of it against her skin was strangely comforting. Was it simply that she could feel? Was that what was happening to her in this strange eclipse of fractured, fragmented family that would soon be orbiting around Chloe and her child? Her legs had their own momentum as she headed for St Kilda Road with its wide boulevard into the city. Trams sped by in quick succession. She could climb aboard one at any time. What was it that she was hurrying towards while ensuring she did not get there too early?

* * *

Her phone rang with the melodic music of wind chimes. She picked it hurriedly off the table and answered.

"Anna?" His voice sounded strained.

"Yes Dad."

"Do you think you can get off early, join me at the hospital to visit your sister?"

"I'm not at work. I didn't feel up to it. I've taken some days off." She laughed nervously. "I'm in the city. Tell me when you're going and I'll be there." She was nestled at a table in the back of a café in Collins Street. She had walked much of the way to the city and then jumped on a tram to ride the rest of the way in.

She had disembarked and visited a bookshop, browsing for as long as she felt she could in the near empty store, while trying to avoid the well-meaning ministrations of a chatty salesgirl. Finally she had settled on a medium sized paperback that she could carry about easily in her handbag. She had found a comfortable looking café with pleasant staff and had seated herself at a back table and attempted to read, but she read the same lines over and over again and somehow failed to grasp their meaning. The words would not penetrate her brain, refused to lodge there or make any sense. She gave up at last and made a show of reading; it protected her from the need for any unwanted conversation, be it with staff or fellow customers, while she waited

68

for the courage or motivation to move. Her father's call gave her both. She need not face this alone after all.

The café owner smiled at her as she approached the till to pay for her coffee and leave. He was Italian, in his mid-fifties. He was joking with his wife as she walked away from the counter with a fully laden breakfast tray to serve the only other customers, a young couple sitting at a window table. As he took Anna's money he noticed that her hand shook slightly and just how pale she was. He handed her the change. "Are you alright, miss?"

"Yes, thank you, I'm fine." She smiled at him with as much warmth as she could muster and reached for the door. She slipped slightly and righted herself.

He opened the door for her. "Well, have a good day then."

She could see he did not believe her. It was as if her usual blinkers had been stripped from her and she could not help but discern more clearly; concern expressed by a stranger, ordinary human kindness, they emphasised what was missing in her life.

* * *

The glass doors of the ground floor lobby opened and she rose to greet him. He was more casually dressed, in woollen trousers, a sports jacket, and open-necked shirt, but he was elegant, always elegant, it was innate in his stance, his movements. She knew it was something she had inherited from him, and it was the thing her mother perhaps despised the most in each of them. She hurried towards him.

He kissed her on the cheek. "Thank you, Anna, this is not an easy thing for me to do." He reached for her hand and squeezed it briefly then let it drop. "I appreciate your support. I won't forget it."

She wanted to take his hand and cling to it in gratitude, to find the strength in it that she needed and longed for. But even more she wanted to shout at him. "You! You! This is not all about you! I'm here, this is tearing at me. Don't you see? Can't you for once see me?"

She stood silently beside him. He began to walk towards the lifts and she walked with him. Yesterday he would not ring Chloe while she was staying with her mother, because he might have to hear her mother's voice and then decide if he would speak or not. Today he was braving an actual encounter, after decades. Was it about Chloe, the child who was forbidden him? Was it to do with his unfulfilled longing for a son that Louis at times seemed to satisfy in some small measure? Did he want to sight this grandson before he too might slip away, become a ghost of possibility lost, never to be spoken of again? Would that happen to Daniel, as it had to Anton? It seemed unlikely given how they were gathering here to acknowledge him. Her jealousy began to rise and she fought hard to grapple with it.

It was all so confusing. Daniel had two parents who would both see him today. Was it her father and mother she was raging at inside or Louis? Why wasn't he here with her, why couldn't he see the chance for some amends in this? Must she always face life's tragedies like some adult child with no partner beside them to count on, just as her parents had for most of their lives? No, today it would seem she must play parent to her father. Was it a version of this that she had lived out all these years with Louis?

"Anna, it's the seventh floor. We need to get out."

She stared at him blankly. She had not been aware of entering the lift with him. He was pressing the button that held the lift doors open and waiting for her to exit first. She could feel herself unravelling. Nearly twelve months of silence, fortitude, denial: would it all collapse in some turgid scene where she might disgrace and shame herself? She pulled herself upright and stepped from the lift.

Finally she noticed the people. They had been there in the busy lobby and in the corridors as she and her father had navigated their way to the lifts. How had she seen them but not noticed them? The hospital was awake and bustling where last night it had been empty, dormant. The seventh floor was alive with receptionists, nursing sisters, patients, parents, visitors. She felt dazed. It reminded her forcibly of the opening scene from *My Fair Lady* which she had gone to with both her parents as a child. It was as if all these people had somehow walked on stage in different time frames and had suddenly sprung to life before her; and flowers, everywhere large bouquets and flower arrangements on the move, or so it seemed, as someone delivering flowers left the lift with them.

She must gain control of herself, be of use. It was her place in the family and a role that had enabled her to function at times when Chloe had simply dissolved into chaos or despair. She had never had that luxury, or had feared the consequences too greatly, or had clung to hope more strongly—she really didn't know which and there was no point in trying to make sense of it. But it was not happening this time. Something strange and disturbing was going on; far from taking charge she was struggling to think clearly at all.

"Anna? This way." Her father was some metres from her, smiling acknowledgement at the hospital clerk behind the reception desk and gesticulating up the corridor. "She's in room seventeen. With any luck we'll have her to ourselves."

He was marching ahead of her in his sprightly, energetic way. She hurried to catch up and with effort matched his pace, walking beside him until they stopped at the door of room seventeen. It was slightly ajar. No sound emanated from the room. They both paused and in that hesitation was a modicum of fear that surfaced just so briefly, yet she noticed it and knew that it was shared. He walked in ahead of her and she followed close behind. They were alone with Chloe. There she lay, propped up on pillows, more lustre in her hair, more colour in her face, eyes closed, head turned away, her profile strangely peaceful. She looked so ethereal, so lovely, and so sad.

He stood by her for a moment then gently reached for her hand and held it. She opened her eyes and they filled with tears that spilled silently down her face. "Dad, oh Dad." Her voice was plaintive, like a young child's cry on waking. He lent forward and kissed her softly on the forehead.

Anna felt like an intruder. She ought not to be here in this moment of intimacy; far greater than any her sister and father had shared since her sister's early childhood. She wished she had not witnessed it. She longed to back away before she too was seen, but she knew she could not. He would soon remember she was present; she doubted she was being asked to play audience on this occasion: far more likely she had simply been forgotten. He sat on the bed beside Chloe, still holding her hand. Anna looked past them through the large windows at the city buildings and the grey sky.

"Have you heard anything more, sweetheart, about your little boy?" His voice was gentle, soothing.

Chloe shook her head silently from side to side. "Adrian and I will be going to see him later this afternoon, once I get all of this out." She nodded at the intravenous line that was bandaged to her other hand, and Frederick followed it with his eyes to the bag of fluid suspended on a metal pole on the other side of the bed from him.

His gaze lingered on the slow drip, drip, drip, from the bag to the tube. "How are you feeling? Are you in pain?"

"No, I have a tube in my back for pain relief. The anaesthetist is coming to take it out before I'm allowed to go wondering about the hospital."

Anna couldn't bear it. Had he ever asked her such a question in her entire life? They were oblivious to her existence, let alone presence. "You can't have an intra-spinal catheter. They wouldn't have had time to put one in with a cord prolapse!" Her voice sounded harsh, her words awkward, jarring.

"Annie?" Chloe looked at her bewildered. "Did you just get here?"

Anna didn't answer. She stood at the foot of the bed, looking at her sister intently.

She dare not speak again until she had won the battle with the intense feeling of disgust for Chloe that was surging within her, for in that moment her sister repulsed her. She had a sudden surge of nausea, beads of perspiration broke out on her face, and she felt light-headed. She had never fainted in her life but the symptoms fitted with a vasovagal reaction, so she forced herself into the chair beside the bed and sat down heavily. She leant forward in the chair, the waves of nausea that buffeted her stirring a deep rage within. Why was her body betraying her now? Her father and Chloe looked at her in silent confusion, seemingly unable to fathom her strange and unaccustomed behaviour.

"Chloe?" Adrian stood at the entrance to the room with a look of utter contempt on his face. He disliked Anna intensely at the best of times, but Frederick even more so, no, in truth, he loathed them. There sat Anna spilling forward from her seat so close to Chloe; Anna with her rock star boyfriend and her thinly veiled dislike of him. She was so unlike her mother in character, much as she resembled her in looks. Felicity was civilised. She may not like Ballarat or be religious, but she had made no attempt to dissuade Chloe from her life with him or her new-found devotion and he knew that in her he and Chloe always had a place to stay, someone to call if in need; she knew how to behave. Anna on the other hand was unpredictable and moody. She kept trying to reach some place in Chloe that he knew nothing about.

As for their father, he was like a being from another universe, so alien was he from anything or anyone Adrian had ever known. They had met twice briefly and Adrian had found no common language with which to communicate, despite Frederick's attempts to put him at his ease. He despised Frederick for his own ineptness in his presence. In truth he knew neither of them at all as people in their own right.

They were more objects from Chloe's past that he wished he could free her from, disengage whatever hold they still had on her; relegate them to oblivion. He thought he had succeeded, at least with Frederick, but there he sat on the bed beside her, holding her hand like some doting, much loved father.

Anna pulled herself upright to a seated position as soon as she heard Adrian. She would not have him see her vulnerability. Her nausea subsided dramatically in the few intense seconds that he stood at the door glaring at them in silence. Anna looked past him at the tall earnest couple standing awkwardly behind him. Their faces looked both eager and embarrassed. She addressed them instead of Adrian.

"Violet, Phillip, this is my father Frederick Mason. Dad, meet Violet and Phillip Hargraves, Adrian's parents."

The Hargraves moved swiftly into the room, passing their son as though he had no substance, their attention completely focused on Frederick. It was as if Chloe and Anna too, had ceased to exist. They were quiet-living, well-educated country teachers in their mid-fifties. They had married young and had their children in their twenties. They were deeply embedded in the community provided by their Church, their work, and their township. A trip to Melbourne to see a special play or musical performance was a fondly remembered highlight in their lives. Somewhere they had accepted that a person as famous as Frederick Mason was not someone they should ever meet. The fact that his daughter was married to their son made no difference to this, especially as the Chloe they knew appeared to have no discernible connection to her father.

Phillip extended his hand to Frederick, who had climbed off the bed and was standing bedside it. Frederick shook the offered hand warmly, then leant forward and kissed Violet on the cheek with a casual assurance and lightness that gave not the slightest hint he had noticed their eagerness. "It is such a pleasure to meet you both at last. I understand you have been extremely kind to my Chloe." He glanced at Chloe with deep affection as he spoke and brought her to their focus in a different way, linked as she now was with him. "It is a great relief to me to think that she will have your support and care at this critical time, for her and for our grandson Daniel."

Anna stared at her father in wonderment. So deft, so amazingly simple, a few words and these people he might never have met had the birth gone well were suddenly linked by a bond of kinship to him; their mutual grandson, a bond so great that she could see they would now do even more for Chloe, not just for her sake, not Adrian's nor Daniel's, but for his as well. How did he do it?

Violet Hargraves looked sadly from Frederick to Chloe. She grasped Chloe's right hand with both of her own. "Poor little soul, truly in the lion's den. We have spoken with Reverend Withers, special prayers are being said for him." She squeezed Chloe's hand, but uncharacteristically, Chloe did not respond, her hand lay limp in those of her mother-in-law. Violet looked at her with surprise and hurt, but Chloe would not meet her gaze. She looked instead past Violet to her father. Frederick did not see her looking at him. He was intent on a conversation with Phillip, about Melbourne and how much it had changed since his last visit.

Anna felt a sudden pang of fear for Chloe; she was far too fragile, did not have the strength for this deep connection, this glimpse of another world that their father might offer but had never been able to sustain. He would be gone in a few days and these others in the room, whatever their limitations, were the ones who would be there to help Chloe struggle though the days and years ahead. To see their blandness in her father's presence could bring only a keen glimpse of the cage she had chosen to protect herself, far better not to see it at all.

Adrian felt his hands tremble and clenched them into fists, all colour drained from his already pale skin. He was livid. The small room was filled with noise and talk and all present, save perhaps Anna, who barely counted, paying homage to a man he could not abide; his wife, his child, his place at the centre of this apparently forgotten. In a few steps he was on the other side of the bed, but the intravenous stand in his way meant he was only level with Chloe's legs. He grabbed clumsily at her bandaged hand and she sat forward startled by the pain of pressure on the cannula in her vein. She turned to him, her eyes filled with surprise and hurt. She looked so vulnerable, so childlike and beautiful, he wished he could drive all these others away, his parents included, and find a quiet place to curl up with her, to shelter her from what lay ahead of them. His anger receded and he was left with nothing to sustain him. He slid silently to sit on the foot of her bed, his head bowed.

Frederick looked at him with pity. "Come, Anna. Let's give Adrian and his parents some time with Chloe. There must be somewhere here we can have a cup of tea?"

He smiled at Chloe and kissed her lightly on the cheek. "I'll come back after that and see if you know when and if it might be possible for me to visit your little boy."

"We will be seeing him first!" Adrian spat the words at him and his parents and Chloe stared at him with surprise.

"It might be tomorrow, Dad. Will you come again tomorrow?" Chloe's voice was soft but her tone was urgent. She spoke as if she was alone in the room with him.

"Of course I will, sweetheart. Would you rather we leave it at that for today?"

She looked at him and nodded silently.

He touched Adrian on the shoulder and held out his hand to him. Adrian took it awkwardly. "Look after her, my boy. I'll see you all soon." He smiled at everyone in the room and headed for the door. A brief glance in Anna's direction indicated undeniably that she should follow. She rose, nodded at Chloe and Adrian's parents in parting, avoided any acknowledgement of Adrian, and left in her father's wake. She hated herself for this loss of autonomy or volition, but she could not resist his summons; it paired with her fear of being left alone in a room filled with Hargraves, for that was what Chloe had become.

She was surprised to find him waiting for her outside the room instead of having to chase after him as she had anticipated. It helped revive some sense of self-respect. They walked away from the room in silence. Then he spoke, his voice unusually serious. "They're far more capable than their son. I hope they are good to her."

"I'm sure they mean to be. They are certainly very present in Chloe and Adrian's lives; you know, daily phone calls or visits. Their daughter is studying in Adelaide. I think Chloe's taken her place." Her voice was flat. "But I'm pretty sure Chloe speaks to Mum daily too."

"She needs that much support?"

"I guess so." It was one way of looking at it, and perhaps true. She had always thought it a symptom of Chloe's inability to say no to their mother, to lay claim to her own life that now extended to her relationship with her in-laws.

Concern, concern for Chloe, it was surely fair enough, they had just left her in a hospital bed, her child might not survive, but was this all there was for her, to be her father's source of information about her sister's life? She looked straight ahead, her eyes unseeing as she walked along beside him. Tomorrow she would come alone. She wanted to see Daniel, but not with him. She felt his hand grab her arm and press it tightly.

"Don't leave me alone with her!" His voice was hushed but urgent.

She started into awareness of her surroundings and saw her mother stepping out of the lift ten metres from them. But her mother appeared not to see her at all. Her eyes were fixed on her father. It alarmed her.

"Frederick." The word was almost a caress.

* * *

"What do you think, Annie? What if I wait till they've both had breakfast and they're both in really good moods? Today's the best chance to try, don't you think? Can you ask for me? Please?" Chloe was hopping about from one foot to the other with excitement.

"Stop it, Chloe! I can't hear what's going on." They were both still in their pyjamas, the TV was on, and Anna was trying to focus on her favourite cartoon.

Chloe jumped directly in front of Anna, put her hands on her sister's knees, placed her face in her line of vision and made her eyes go cross-eyed.

"Okay, you're hilarious!" Anna tried to sound angry but Chloe was a lovable clown who knew how to get her attention.

"Promise you'll ask and I'll get out of the way."

"No, I'm not going to ask. I can't do everything for you all the time." Chloe pouted at her in response. Anna went on. "Anyway, I think there's a much better chance they'll say yes if you ask. Try Dad first, there's no way he'd say no!"

Chloe stood up and thought for a moment, her head held to one side. She straightened it suddenly and her curls bobbed violently about. "I'll ask Mum first. She might just get cross if Daddy says yes. More chance it'll happen if it's her choice."

Anna looked at her sister with new-found respect. "You're probably right."

Chloe began to do a strange little dance around the room with an imaginary violin and bow. Anna watched her keenly. Of course they would say yes. Dad would just love it that Chloe wanted to learn the violin. Mum would probably complain about taking her to lessons but she would be proud to have a little girl who could play such a difficult instrument. Anna felt a small, sharp sting of jealousy.

Sunday was the best day of the week by far. Their father was often at home. Both parents usually slept in and they were free to watch TV and play in the lounge and family rooms without any instructions from their mother on what they should be doing. Best of all their parents were sometimes happy together on a Sunday morning and their father might even play with them for a while. Anna focused on the TV again. She tried to work out what was happening to Scooby-Doo and his friends as they solved another mystery but suddenly the high energy action and music seemed too much. Maybe Mum was right and she was too old for cartoons. She turned the TV off and Chloe stopped her dance and looked at Anna in surprise. She seized her chance. "Want to get changed and play outside in the cubby?"

"Okay, but don't go thumping around and wake them up."

Chloe bolted up the stairs to change and Anna followed her more cautiously. It did not matter who made the noise, their mother always blamed her, either for making it or for not keeping Chloe quiet.

The cubby-house at the bottom of their garden had been built by their father of solid oak boards that had come from the floor of a demolished house in the neighbourhood. It was an amazing thing that he should have built it for them at all, for he never showed his capability as a handyman in any other way. It was a wondrous place in itself. It had a built-in wooden bar that served as their kitchen and it was lined with shelves that had been filled with Anna's much loved china tea set, many of their favourite books, and an exotic array of dolls that their father had brought back for them from his trips abroad. Their mother had sewn curtains for the windows and had let them have an odd assortment of unwanted plastic bowls and spoons, as well as some old pans. There were two small wooden chairs, a pile of colouring books, pencils and crayons, and a blackboard with coloured chalk. It was their refuge where they could play for hours if it was clear they had best not disturb their mother.

They took a packet of shortbread biscuits with them and a bottle of lemonade from the fridge and after a solid hour of imaginary play and real morning tea Anna was reading *Black*

Beauty and Chloe was colouring a large picture of flowers and butterflies. Chloe lifted her head at once in alarm at the sound of raised angry voices and shouting. Anna, absorbed in her book seemed not to hear. Chloe rushed to her sister's side, clasped her arm, and shook it. "Annie, I'm scared. It's Mum and Dad."

Anna stopped reading and immediately heard the harsh adult voices. How could it be their parents? They never shouted at each other. Their mother was often annoyed with them and spoke loudly if she wanted something done, but she never shouted and it was simply inconceivable that she would do so at their father. Anna prised her sister's hand from her arm and held it in hers. "We'll go together, Chloe, but stay next to me all the time and don't make any noise. Understand?"

Chloe nodded wordlessly in response and held her big sister's hand tightly as they crept through the garden towards the kitchen door.

The kitchen window was open and the voices rang out through the neighbourhood. "You think you can do this do you? Have sex with me after being with some fucking whore?" Their mother was shrieking. Anna's heart was racing and Chloe's fingers were digging into her hand as she held on tighter.

"She's no whore, Felicity! For Christ sake, keep your voice down!"

"Why? Afraid the neighbours will know about the real Frederick fucking Mason!"

"I was thinking about the girls."

Their mother began to laugh hysterically. Anna opened the door as silently as she could and peeked through a slit. Their mother was standing with one of their father's shirts in her hand by the kitchen sink and he was a long way away from her at the door that came off the family room.

"Were you thinking of the girls when you did this?" Felicity held the shirt up towards him. She threw the shirt to the floor and turned to the sink, then spun back around to face Frederick.

She was holding up a large kitchen knife. It happened so fast that Anna felt stunned and disbelieving. There was a piercing shriek as Chloe poked her head past Anna and saw her mother. Felicity dropped the knife and it clattered to the floor not far from her foot. She picked up a dinner plate from the sink and threw it with all her might at the back door and her daughters. Anna pulled back and slammed the door as the plate clattered into it. Chloe was clinging to her, trembling and sobbing. Anna hugged her sister and realised that Chloe had wet herself.

* * *

Anna felt shock and distress. Her heartbeat began to race and pound, her chest felt tight and she feared she would not be able to speak if she needed to because her throat was strangely constricted. A voice in her head told her these were symptoms of panic undoubtedly associated with the violent verbal battles she had witnessed between her parents as a child. How long had these raged for? She had no idea. She remembered the first time vividly but it had taken months for her parents to separate and the fights had continued. The rational knowledge did nothing to stave off her reaction. She focused on her stomach and tried to change to deep abdominal breathing. She and her father stood still while her mother approached them with slow, measured steps. Anna visualised her mother reaching them, reverting to the rage that ordinarily informed any reference to her father, and slapping either him or her forcibly on the face: the fantasy alternated at this point.

Her mother stopped immediately in front of her father. She was as tall as him in her high heels and stared searchingly into his eyes. Anna found it completely unnerving, but sensed her father suddenly grow calm.

"I wish I could say time's been kind."

How could he say such a thing to her mother? Anna looked and saw her mother's face, lined as it was with the bitterness and discontent of many years, but her usual disdain was absent; instead she wore an expression that was completely unfamiliar: oddly softer, sadder than Anna could have imagined possible.

"It has to you, Frederick. You look exactly the same."

This was bizarrely unexpected. Anna didn't trust it. Her fantasy changed to something akin to a Batman movie she had once seen, in which her mother came in close only to throw acid into her father's face in a pique of sadistic envy. Her father's strange confidence continued however. It was as if he sensed that the woman before him could no longer harm him, had lost any power to do so, and that her mother grasped this too in some wordless way.

Her mother turned to face her. "So you've taken him to see Chloe? Judas!"

"Leave her alone, Felicity. I asked her to come with me." He spoke kindly to Anna. "Why don't you go home? I'll call you tomorrow. Your mother and I need to talk."

Anna left her parents without a word of farewell. She hurried to the lift with a longing to be far away from both of them. The lift was full and she stood to one side, enjoying the company of strangers who would ask nothing of her, mean nothing to her, who could provoke no intense thought or feeling. She sped through the ground floor foyer and out into the street. The pavement was quiet, and a cold wind whipped about her. She stopped for a moment, dazed by the brightness of the winter sun in mid-afternoon. She orientated herself as she stared at the broad road and the construction works going on opposite the hospital, then turned towards Royal Parade to head for her tram stop and the start of her journey home. She felt a sudden surge of freedom, a strange sense of elation. He had stood up for her. Unprecedented, unbidden, something never recognisable in its absence but perhaps longed for all her life. Let them sort it out together, it was none of her business, it never had been.

* * *

She turned her key in the door. The lights were on and the heating: he must be home. "That was quick!" Charlie's voice from a distance, his words slightly slurred.

She called out in response. "It's Anna!" Shit! She'd have to be civil. She glanced around the house as she walked towards the kitchen, habitually checking if things were in order, in a fit state for visitors. She stood in the doorway staring down at Charlie as he sat at the table, a bottle of beer in his hand, shirtsleeves rolled up, and a broad smile on his round face. He was starting to look very middle-aged; his dirty blond hair was mingled with grey and thinning, he was even developing a beer belly. She noticed the wine stains on the table just in front of his hand. Damn Louis! He hadn't bothered to clean them.

Against her will she had always liked Charlie, but had dreaded his visits to her house which inevitably meant that Louis would be off somewhere on tour very soon. Now it felt like a reprieve. So much had changed in a few days.

"Hi Charlie. Where's he gone?"

"Good to see you too, Anna! Long time and all of that." His eyes were bright with mirth. Then he remembered. "Sorry, love, Louis told me about your sister's kid. I just forgot. He's off to get some supplies. We have a great tour to plan."

She gave him a strange smile. "I thought as much. You two won't want me in the midst of your planning session. If you'll excuse me, I need a nap, I'm really bushed. Could you ask Louis not to wake me? I'll be in the spare bedroom."

He looked at her oddly. "Don't give up on him, Anna. I don't know how he'll make it without you."

It took her by surprise. Charlie was always so laid back with her, he would never acknowledge any of the underlying conflict in their own relationship, let alone venture into what went on between Louis and her.

"I don't know what Louis's told you, but it's okay with me this time, Charlie. It's fine, really. You won't get any opposition, competition, none of it. Those days are over."

He looked at her with alarm. He sounded hurt. "Don't know what you're on about, Anna, I've always been your greatest fan. Louis changed completely for you, sobered up. It'll shred him if you leave him, he won't cope."

"You overestimate my importance." Her voice was soft and weary. "You don't know how little there is left between us. Anyway he's far from sober now." She turned to go.

"You have no idea do you? He was in real trouble before he met you." He looked about him furtively, as if he feared Louis should overhear somehow. "He'd kill me if he finds out I told you, but I figure it's time you know. His Mum died a few months before he met you."

She had turned back to face him and nodded with growing impatience: she knew this.

"But it was Stella and the abortion that really shattered him. She did it the week after his Mum died."

Anna stood riveted, alert and frightened.

Charlie looked at her with pity. "I figured he hadn't told you. She had the abortion, then told him that she'd done it. She hadn't told him she was pregnant, he had no chance to have his say. I've never seen him so angry. He never spoke to her again, went on the biggest bender possible. Had us all so worried. Then six months later he met you and he sobered right up, became the Louis we'd known from years ago. Bloody marvellous, miraculous."

She was staring straight ahead, looking dazed.

"And you should have seen him in the States. He was so excited, so keen to get his big break over there, so you'd be proud, so he'd have something really big when he became a father. Something big for you and his son ..." His voice trailed off.

"But it meant he wasn't here. He didn't come back for the funeral. He's never been to Anton's grave. He won't even talk to me about him. He's so angry with me." Her voice was choked with tears. She was banging her head lightly but repeatedly against the doorpost.

He stared at her with fear. He stood, unsure if he should go to her and try to comfort her. "Anna, Anna … See the way I figure he's just confused, about you and Stella."

She pulled away from the doorpost and looked at him strangely. "Christ Charlie! Something as important as this and he never told me! Who have I been with? What kind of relationship have we had? I could see how he was when I met him. I thought he was grieving for his Mum, she'd been sick for so long. I guess that one's true? And that his Dad died when he was nine?"

"Don't, Anna, don't. I've really made a mess of this. I've said it all wrong."

"What have you said wrong, mate?" Louis stood in the corridor a few metres behind Anna, a bag filled with takeaway food hanging from one arm and a carton of beer held firmly in the other. He glanced from Anna leaning against the doorpost to Charlie standing in front of the table. Both were pale and upset. He looked directly at Anna. His voice was terse. "Get it straight; this is my decision, not Charlie's. I need this tour! I'm losing it hanging around here all the time. If things are rough at that hospital with your family trying to play at being something they're not, you've no right to come back here and take it out on Charlie!"

She stared at him, silent, strangely calm. "Sure, I've got it." She made to pass him in the corridor then hesitated and turned to look at Charlie. "It's okay, Charlie, you're not the one who's messed anything up. As you see, we're doing a fine job all on our own. Good luck with the tour."

"Fucking superior bitch!" He whispered it in her ear as she passed him, his breath sour with alcohol.

Her eyes filled with tears but her back straightened and she held herself erect, rigid, as she walked steadily away.

FIVE

"Chloe, are you alone?"

"Annie?"

"I'm here in the hospital. Are you alone?"

"Yes, Adrian's gone to lunch, but he'll be back soon."

"Okay, I'll be there in a minute."

She put her phone away hurriedly. She felt like a spy or fugitive slinking down the corridors hoping not to be seen, or maybe just like someone who felt she had no right to be there. She didn't want to meet any of them; not the Hargraves or Adrian, equally not either of her parents. Her father had not rung her as he said he would. She knew the call would come, he always kept his word. But she half dreaded it.

She entered the room. Chloe was sitting up in a chair by the window, completely free of all tubing and attachments. She looked different, far more alert, alive, and tougher, that was it, tougher than she had looked for years, maybe ever. Her habitual cloak of fear and confusion was missing.

"Come in, Annie, don't stand at the door. This is terribly hard for you isn't it?" Concern for her from Chloe? She walked slowly towards her sister.

Chloe nodded towards the bed. "Why don't you sit on the bed? It's so good to be out of it."

"How is he, Chloe? Have you seen him?"

"Yes, Adrian and I saw him yesterday afternoon, and Mum and Dad and Phillip and Violet saw him this morning." Her voice was so matter of fact, as if she was describing some routine outing.

"Mum and Dad?"

"Not together." Chloe gave a strange high laugh. "What happened with them? Were you there? … Mum came to see me yesterday afternoon about an hour after you and Dad left. She was so odd, distracted, I thought she was worried about Daniel. But Dad was here this morning; he said they'd had a cup of tea together, after all these years … a cup of tea …"

"I wasn't there. He asked me to leave as soon as she arrived."

Chloe sighed. "But you want to know about Daniel … he's doing surprisingly well … that's what the doctors say … he wants to live. They think he's going to make it but they don't know how well he'll be as yet." Chloe was calm, so calm, in this most extreme of situations. It was eerily unexpected.

Chloe looked at her sister with sudden earnestness. "I've been praying for him Annie, praying for him every minute I've been on my own. Perhaps there is a greater purpose in his suffering, don't you see, it's brought Mum and Dad together at last, they've been able to talk to one another. Would you have thought that possible? I just can't see how God could let someone as beautiful and innocent as him suffer more than he has already. I'm sure he'll be alright."

Anna took a rasping breath that caught in her chest. Wasn't Anton beautiful and innocent? He had died. She wanted to shout at her sister, to shake her out of her complacent delusion and the self-satisfied sense of meaning she had managed to find. But what would she be left with then?

"Can I see him, Chloe? Are you okay with that? I won't stay long."

"Of course, Annie, I want you to. Do you want to go on your own?" Chloe looked at her earnestly with an unspoken plea that Anna might want her to be present.

"If you don't mind." Anna did not meet her sister's eyes or see her disappointment.

"Just pass me the notebook and pen in the drawer over there, will you? I need to give you a note to say it's okay if you're going on your own." Chloe wrote the note hurriedly and handed it to Anna. She tried to engage her sister once more. "You know you can come and visit us as much as you like when we get home."

Anna stood by her sister's side, the note held tight in one hand. She turned to go and was surprised to feel Chloe clutch at the other.

"I've prayed for Anton every day since he was born too, Annie. I pray for his soul."

Anna leant forward and hugged her sister awkwardly. Displays of affection were rare between them. "Thank you for remembering him, for caring." Her voice was choked by tears that she fought urgently to stop, not now, not with Chloe. She stood and reached for the box of tissues on the cabinet beside the bed. She dabbed at her face hurriedly and turned to take her leave. Adrian stood in the doorway glaring at her with annoyance. There she was again with her histrionics. Anyone would think it was her baby in distress. Chloe was coping far better than he ever thought she could have at such a terrible time and here was her sister falling apart with her own unresolved grief. He felt a sudden unfamiliar pang of pity for her: she had lost a son a year ago; he had a momentary glimmer of the sorrow that might entail, but he pushed it from him, he had no space for this woman, she frightened him too much.

"It's alright, Adrian, I'm just leaving." Anna passed him with the briefest nod in his direction. She couldn't stomach any more of their usual unpleasantness with one another. She knew she would not dissolve into tears again in Adrian's presence; she would simply never forgive herself if she did. All well and good for Chloe to make her so welcome in her home, but it was a home that came with this mean-spirited, possessive man and with their mother's presence always imminent, not a place she would ever feel safe to frequent. But then was anywhere safe? Her own home had become a hostile place too. She had felt so grateful that Louis had ignored her and continued his meeting with Charlie last evening, that he had let her sleep undisturbed in their spare room, and such profound relief that morning when she left without seeing him. There was no escaping the current reality that her life had become some battleground where it seemed essential to dodge the people who were supposed to be closest to her.

* * *

Anna headed for the neonatal intensive care unit feeling far more frightened than she had on the night of Daniel's birth. He was two days old; he'd made it that far, further than Anton. Could she bear to see him or maybe even touch him? She had her sister's permission to actually go in there and find him this time. Would the note be enough to get her in? Chloe seemed to think it would, but Chloe had so little idea about such things, at the best of times, let alone now. She had no head for detail. How did she manage as a primary teacher? Anna was surprised that it had never occurred to her to wonder about this, or much else really about how her sister navigated her life.

She stood in front of the information desk and looked at the woman behind it. She struggled with the urge to turn and walk away. Instead she walked up to the woman. "Hi, I'm Anna Mason. I'm here to see my nephew Daniel Hargraves. I have my sister's written permission." She handed her the note Chloe had written.

"Yes, that's fine, I'll let them know. Just go through."

She waited for the soft buzz of the door release mechanism and pushed the door open.

She had expected to enter a large room, instead she found herself in a long corridor with a warm cream-coloured floor

89

and walls painted with branches and leaves and brightly coloured birds and flowers. She walked past these and past a long mural: pictures of smiling families and babies.

An Asian nurse was walking towards her. "Anna Mason? Hi, I'm Carol, Daniel is just through here." They continued walking down the corridor past closed room after room.

"I had no idea this place was so big."

The nurse smiled but didn't answer until they reached the next room. She pushed the door open. "He's inside this pod."

The room had three closed humidicribs and an open one placed around its four corners. Another nurse and a mother were at the humidicrib furthest away from them. Anna was surprised when Carol led her to the closest one. It was open and the baby in it seemed enormous compared to the other tiny infants in the room. Anna walked towards him slowly, each step measured. She stood half a pace away and stared. She felt a deep sense of shock. What had she expected? He looked so big, but he was just a normal sized, full-term baby. Anton had been more than a month premature. Daniel lay still, breathing silently, tubes in his nostrils but no respirator, soft pink skin, a good sign, a head of blond downy hair. He was so very different to her own small son.

He moved his head just fractionally in his sleep. She grappled with it as she could; he was nothing like Anton. The ache of it was visceral; it caught her just under her diaphragm in the epigastric region, threatened her breathing, landed retrosternally, tightening there, a deep rasping pain. She fought to keep her breathing even and silent, to make sure no one would realise.

"You can stroke his arm if you like." It was the nurse Carol, who was standing beside her. "Here." Anna was surprised to find her still there. She had lost all awareness of anyone and anything but Daniel. The nurse touched Daniel's arm gently, and he moved it, but not in irritation.

Anna felt so frightened to touch him. Her hand reached for him, tentatively at first, felt the silkiness of his baby skin, lingered gently on his arm, touched his shoulder, then reached to stroke his hair. The pain in her chest began to lessen, her breathing eased. He was going to live. He was Daniel.

"That's what he needs. He's doing so well. With any luck we'll have him with his Mum soon."

"Let's hope so, Carol, but I think we may be twenty-four hours away at the earliest." A voice with authority, a familiar male voice. "How are you, Anna?"

The nurse looked from Anna to Matthew with surprise and moved away without further comment.

Anna lifted her hand gently away from Daniel and withdrew it from the humidicrib. She had not consciously thought of Matthew, yet it did not surprise her to hear his voice, so perhaps she had hoped for this meeting. She turned slowly to face him. "I'm much better than I thought I could be." She looked at him steadily, and noticed that his eyes were green not blue as she had imagined. "What's his prognosis, Matthew? Is it any clearer?"

"Guardedly optimistic if speaking to a colleague, hopeful if speaking to a family member, both as far as you're concerned." He smiled at her gently, with concern.

"I'm worried about your sister though, she seems to be … almost happy about his being here, strangely unaware of how dangerous his birth was, what a close thing this has been. I've seen plenty of parents in denial, but there is a childlike quality to her reaction that is really quite concerning. Is she stable these days?"

"What's stable? She's religious!" She looked at him. "That sounds so crass." She glanced at Daniel and away again hurriedly. "I think I need to leave." She met Matthew's eyes: he seemed so solid and sane; she longed for sanity somewhere in her life. "Are you here for much longer?"

"No … I'm just about to go myself. I pick my daughter, Rose, up from school today. I have her for Wednesday nights …" They walked together and as he opened the door of the room for her to exit ahead of him, he spoke to her back. "Would you like to come with me?"

She turned and nodded silently. He smiled at her.

* * *

Anna stared across the narrow road at the hive of energy and life in front of her. Matthew had parked his car on the opposite side of the road but parallel to a metal fence that ran along one side of the schoolyard. She sat absorbed, pleased that she could observe what was happening without being conspicuous in any way herself. It was a playground in an old-fashioned, homely type of infant school that was shaded by large trees and filled with children in purple uniforms, and with parents talking, laughing, picking up children, leading them out by the hand. It was so normal, ordinary, and wonderfully different to the stuff of her life. She could see Matthew quite clearly as he walked through the gate and greeted two mothers who were talking together, then headed for the monkey bars and lifted a small girl with a mop of blonde curls into his arms. The girl hugged him passionately, jumped down, and ran off to return with a purple backpack that he helped hoist onto her shoulders. They walked together hand in hand out of the gate and then stood on the curb not quite opposite the car, waiting to cross. The little girl stared intensely at the car. Anna wondered if she could be seen though the tinted windscreen and windows; she tried to look normal, but felt suddenly and strangely nervous.

They crossed the road and she heard the boot of the car open and close. Then the door behind her opened and Matthew leaned in as his daughter clambered up into the car. "Rose this is Anna, Anna my daughter Rose."

Anna swivelled around to try to see the little girl better. Matthew was adjusting the seat belt over her booster seat.

Rose looked steadily at Anna. "Are you my Dad's girlfriend?"

"Sweetheart, I asked you to go easy didn't I?" Matthew raised his eyebrows and smiled in apology over Rose's head, then shut the door and started walking around the car to the driver's side.

"Are you? It's okay, you can tell me, I won't tell Dad what you say. He needs a girlfriend, he's lonely and Mum's got stinky Bill." Rose giggled.

Anna laughed out loud. "I've heard of Blinky Bill, but not stinky Bill!"

Rose found this simply hilarious and chortled with laughter. Anna continued. "I'm your Dad's friend, well, we're old friends that have just met up after a long time. And I'm a girl."

They heard Matthew's door begin to open.

"I'll ask you again sometime, okay?"

"Okay!"

"What has she got you to agree to in that minute?"

Anna smiled. "Did you say Rose was five? She seems much older than that to me." They heard a loud appreciative giggle from the back seat.

"So where do you live?"

They drove through the streets of Elsternwick, across the Nepean Highway towards the beach.

"Daddy, Molly wouldn't let Ella have her time in the dress-up corner today. She kept taking all the things that Ella wanted."

"Did Ella tell her to stop or ask Miss Edwards to help?"

"No, she couldn't really, 'cause Molly's like that with everyone. Well, all the girls anyway. Jasper tried to help but then Ella told him to go away. I think that was mean, 'cause Jasper likes Ella a lot …" Rose chatted on and on. Her voice sounded like birdsong to Anna: lilting and musical. Anna relaxed and heard, almost against her will, the kindness and genuine interest in Matthew's responses. He wanted to know about his daughter's life; he was deeply invested in understanding her as a person.

"Well here we are. You've been very quiet, are you sure you want to do this?"

Anna looked at him with surprise. The car had stopped. Had they just pulled up or had she been sitting there silently for some time? She felt self-conscious more than embarrassed. She looked at her surroundings and recognised them immediately. They were in a street that bordered a large park and playground in Elwood. It was where she had sometimes met an old school-friend and her son, so that the little boy could play while she and her friend talked. It was set a few streets back from the beach. Matthew lived in the next suburb to her. She had literally been wandering around opposite where he lived, not in the last twelve months, but certainly on at least two occasions in the twelve months prior to that.

"Dropping me off the other night really wasn't out of your way, was it?" She gave a strange laugh.

"I told you, I've seen you around."

"It shouldn't surprise me, nothing should surprise me. Everything is upside down right now."

Rose started giggling loudly. Anna wondered if the little girl thought her actually funny or just odd.

Matthew leaned over and tickled Rose. "Come on, monkey-face." He was out of the car and heading to the back door. He undid Rose's seat belt and she jumped into his arms and was soon perched on his hip.

Anna opened her door cautiously and stood silently next to them. She felt so sombre and subdued especially in the presence of his effervescent little girl. Matthew got the backpack from the boot and started walking towards the entrance to a two storey apartment building. It was a block of four large art deco apartments set back from the road in an established garden. Anna trailed behind them along the garden path as they headed for the recessed porch. She stopped to smell the daphne that was coming into bloom. It reminded her forcibly of the small garden around her farmhouse where she had a well-established bush. Was it in bloom as yet? If so she hadn't noticed at the weekend.

Rose had her hand on Matthew's shoulder and was talking again, in her animated way. Anna wandered up behind them and almost bumped into Matthew who had stopped to unlock the front door to the entrance hall. His sudden unexpected proximity brought a wave of sexual attraction that was completely unexpected, unnerving, and exciting. She stood where she was and did not take the step back that she ordinarily would have. He too lingered a moment longer than necessary, acutely aware of her presence behind him.

Rose turned to look at Anna standing so very close. She reached out and played with Anna's hair. "Dad! Can I watch the *Night Garden*? Then you and Anna can talk."

"Sure, honey." He pushed the door open and moved forward. Anna waited, then followed.

His apartment was upstairs and Anna climbed the stairs slowly. By the time she reached it the door was wide open. Rose had grabbed her backpack and run off to her bedroom. Matthew stood in the doorway watching her. She stopped in front of him, facing him. He reached out and moved a lock of hair gently out of her eyes, caressed the side of her face, his hand moved lightly on down her neck over her shoulders to the spot between her shoulder blades where she loved to be touched. Such easy familiarity, there was no doubt they had once been lovers. She leant forward and brushed his lips with hers, just for a moment before she walked into his apartment.

"You realise I'm unhinged at the moment? I can't vouch for my actions. They've been taking me by surprise all week."

He laughed softly. "I'll take unhinged, it's far better than absent."

He followed her into the apartment and watched her as she stood by the fireplace, her arm on the mantelpiece, studying the room. Had he always imagined her doing this? It seemed so, for the picture she created was so very familiar that he felt unsure if it was a memory of her, or a dream of her. She moved to the window that looked out over the park. The golden winter sunlight played across her features and gave her skin a richer glow than ever truly belonged to her. He imagined her in health and happiness. Was such a thing possible, for either of them, for both?

She turned her head away, her profile lost momentarily, then turned it back to face him with a smile. "It's lovely, the apartment, the view. It's so peaceful here, so quiet. Is it yours?"

"No, I'm renting. I'm hoping to buy a house around here once we sell our place in Brighton and the settlement comes through."

"Our place?"

"Hard habit to break." He gave a dry laugh. "Lord knows why. There's been no real we for a long time, long before Claire and I separated."

"It seems to be the way it goes, doesn't it? It's so much easier to fall into a relationship than out of one."

"Sometimes." He looked at her intently.

She met his gaze. "Why didn't we go on? You remember, tell me."

"I don't really know. I've always told myself I was protecting you from my sadness, but maybe I was just afraid."

"That's candid, if ironic." She laughed softly, but her face was expressionless. "Sadness seems to be my thing. I got together with Louis soon after his mother died. Maybe you weren't messy enough for me. I think I've needed to be a rescuer."

"Past tense?" He lifted an eyebrow at her and smiled.

"I certainly hope so."

"I don't know, we could try and rescue each other?"

Her phone rang and she followed the sound hastily. She walked to the couch where she had tossed her bag, opened it and hurriedly retrieved the phone. She looked at the screen. "Excuse me, I need to take this." She answered the phone as she walked back to the window and turned her back on him.

"Hi Dad, I missed you at the hospital today."

"Well, yes … we missed each other. Are you free for dinner tonight?"

She turned to look at Matthew, but he had left the room. "No, no, I'm sorry, I can't make it. How about breakfast tomorrow? I'll come to your hotel and we can go to the hospital from there."

"Alright, yes that's fine."

She was sure he was checking a schedule or had someone else with him. "How did it go, Dad, you and Mum together, seeing Daniel?"

"I think it best we discuss all that in person tomorrow morning. Would ten suit?"

"Yes, I'll see you in the lobby."

Was there someone with him, or was it simply that she wasn't rushing to be with him as soon as he rang! She felt a surge of anger but it passed in a moment. She didn't care. She was past caring about people who wanted her to live on dregs.

She heard noises and walked into the kitchen that was off the lounge room. Matthew was buttering slices of bread and laying them out in front of him at a granite island-bench in the middle of the room and Rose was perched on a high stool beside him. They were both wearing aprons. Anna laughed out loud. It was so unexpected.

"Anna, come and see! We're making fairy bread." Rose was jiggling about with excitement as Matthew handed her the plastic container full of hundreds and thousands to sprinkle on the buttered bread.

"Fairy bread? I haven't had any since I was … about your age." She smiled broadly at Rose; a smile full of sudden natural warmth.

Matthew cut each slice of bread into four small triangles and the little girl picked up the plate and offered it to Anna with all the anticipation of a hostess. Anna took one of the tiny triangles, covered in its myriad of the rainbow coloured sprinkles, and popped it into her mouth whole. She began to chew with a look of genuine pleasure.

Rose grinned at her, very pleased. "I love fairy bread. Daddy and I make it every Wednesday for afternoon tea. Just so you know where to get some as you like it."

"Thank you, Rose. I'll remember that." Anna smiled at Rose and then at Matthew.

"Join us for dinner, Anna? Nothing fancy, we're making pumpkin pasta." His voice was even, it carried no expectation.

"Yes … that would be lovely. What can I do?"

Anna helped them cook, watched intently as Matthew prepared the simple pasta dish, sat at the table, ate with them, and wondered what she was doing stepping into someone else's life this way. Yet it was so different to what awaited her at home. Their easy relationship was something she had never known in this version, but it reminded her of a playful, tender way of relating that she and her father and Chloe had shared when she was young, when he and her mother were happier. The time passed so quickly.

"Bath and bedtime coming up. So Anna, can we give you a lift home first?" Matthew reached out and touched her hand where it lay on the table.

She let his hand rest against hers for a few moments then moved her hand away, but she smiled at him as she did so. "No, thanks, I'll call a cab. It'll be easier all round." She didn't know if Louis would even be home, but she wanted to keep this separate. She had to do whatever was needed to sort things out with Louis, to end the tortured way they had been existing for the last year; only then could she turn her mind to what might be possible with Matthew. She got out her phone and he assumed she was about to call for a taxi but she turned to him instead. "Can I get your number? Then I can text you mine as well. Don't think I'll be spending too much more time at the Royal Women's."

* * *

The house was dark and cold. He must have been out for most of the day too. Anna switched on the hall light and the heating once she had disarmed the alarm. At least he had remembered to turn that on and to deadlock the doors. Her home, how strange, how bleak it felt after the life and laughter she had just left. How sad Matthew must be on his days without Rose. He'd said that it was hard being with other children all the time and not her. She understood that now, having seen how close they were. Matthew, her head was full of Matthew and Rose. What about her father, her mother, Chloe, Daniel? Most of all what about Louis? They were so desperate, so vile to each other after a year of going through the motions, the pretence of a life together when their bond with each other was broken, fractured by their inability to talk about what mattered most: their son's death and the fact that neither of them had really survived it, if such a thing could be survived. The reality that their relationship was dying was being made so evident with the birth of this other little boy, yet neither of them was making any attempt to reach out, to take hold of the slender thread that might still pull them back towards each other.

She felt again the deep aching that was so familiar, had been so much a part of her this last year, and realised with surprise that she had been free of it, briefly. Somewhere in the time spent with Matthew and Rose it had departed or receded sufficiently so that it no longer defined her capacity to relate to everything. She took a long, slow breath; it was possible to be at least partially free. She realised she was standing with her head against the wall just inside the front door. She walked into the bedroom that had been hers and Louis's in all their years together. The bed was unmade, his clothes were draped on the chair by his side, a pile of his shoes was under the dressing table. She went to their chest of drawers and took out underwear and pyjamas. She got the clothes she wanted for the next day from the wardrobe.

She walked slowly along the corridor and stopped at the door of the little room next to theirs. She turned the doorknob, opened the door, and turned on the light. It was such a cheerful little room; painted blue with a yellow and white frieze of dancing clowns and bears just above the skirting board. A large white wooden cot stood in the middle of the room with a mobile of seagulls suspended over it, Louis's choice. There was a long wooden chest against the far wall just beneath the window with its creamy blind, and the change table stood in one corner. She felt her chest tighten and tears begin to burn behind her eyes but she walked into the room for the first time in how many months? She touched the blankets in the cot and picked up a small brown teddy bear that lay on the pillow. She stroked its head and put it down again. She knelt in front of the chest and placed the pile of her own belongings on the floor beside her.

* * *

The window was wide open and the little room was bathed in light and getting hotter by the minute. Neither of them cared. The heat had dried the paint earlier than expected and the light breeze that wafted in helped with the acrid smell. Anna was kneeling by the wall closest to the door, measuring and carefully cutting the wallpaper for the frieze to the right length. Louis was on a ladder by the window hanging the pale cream blind. Anna grunted suddenly and sat on the floor cross legged.

"Louis, come quickly!"

He had just slipped the blind into its brackets and was about to try it out. He looked down at her with concern. "What's wrong?"

She laughed. "No, no. You have to come and feel this. He's doing gymnastics or kicking a goal."

He climbed down the ladder hurriedly and knelt beside her. She took his hand and placed on the side of her swollen abdomen underneath her long maternity smock. His hand moved and he laughed with surprise as it was pummelled repeatedly by a tiny foot. He lifted the smock and watched for the movement that might give him a glimpse of the size or shape of his little son's foot. He sat in front of her and bent forward and kissed her distended belly.

"Lord, honey, that's amazing, truly amazing. Can't imagine how it must feel, having him moving around inside you like that all the time." There was a look of complete wonder on his face. He leant forward and this time kissed her tenderly on the lips, the softest of kisses. "Thank you."

She looked at him bemused, uncertain. "What are you thanking me for?"

He looked away momentarily, a wave of emotion overwhelming him. He looked back and smiled as he brushed her cheek gently. "For being so clever, so fabulous, for having our baby!"

She reached forward and placed a hand on either side of his face. She looked at him squarely and smiled. "Truly, my pleasure." But she could not hold the intense, almost pleading look that met hers. It was too much for her in some way. She lowered her eyes and her hands at the same time and turned slightly. She picked up the strip of wallpaper. "Help me with this?"

They began to apply it to the wall, working together, she rolling it into place after he applied the paste and then smoothing it with her finger tips; finally they both worked over it with dry brushes to remove any bubbles. She sighed lightly with appreciation. "It looks so beautiful. He's going to love it."

He laughed at her softly. "The important thing is you already do!"

* * *

She raised the lid of the chest to a point where it would stay open. She knelt motionless and gazed at the contents. Slowly, reverently she lowered her hand into it and lifted out a pale blue top with a little white sailboat embroidered on it. She let it drape and fall across her uplifted palm; so small, so exquisite.

She had imagined taking him down to watch the boats from St Kilda pier dressed in this. Tears began to roll down her face and she let them. She placed the top back in the chest and took instead a little china photo frame with knots of purple flowers on its face and an oval window that was empty. She picked up her handbag and took out a small striped notebook held together with a rubber band. She took off the rubber band and let the book fall open. There it was; a photo of Anton taken just after they turned off the respirator and took out the tube. She couldn't bear to keep it on her phone. She had saved it onto her computer and had printed this copy. She kept it with her always, but never looked at it.

She turned the little frame over and removed the back. She placed the photo in it and turned it over again, a perfect fit. She slid the back of the frame into place and fastened the little clips. She took a long look at him: his eyes were closed, he could be sleeping, he was just so beautiful. Her chest and her throat ached so much she could hardly bear it. She began to sob, deep racking sobs that shook her body; she let them come and clutched the frame to her chest. She had no idea how long she had been crying but finally it stopped. She closed the chest, picked up her own clothes, and stood. She hesitated, then turned and walked from the room, turning off the light and closing the door behind her.

Once in the guest room she placed the photo in its frame on the bedside table. She was not going to hide him away any more. If Louis had never been able to look at him that was his problem. No, she didn't need to blame Louis. She was tired of that bitterness. Something in her was changing and there was freedom in it. She sat on the single bed and glanced around the guest room. What was she doing holed up in one room of her own home? In case Louis came back? They had barely spoken in days. In the time just after Anton's death it had been so difficult to speak at all, yet Louis had still rung her on some days until he finally made it home from the States; his son dead and his plans for international success gone. She looked at her mobile phone where it lay on the bed next to the pile of clothes. She could pick it up and phone him in an instant. But something in her hardened and would not let her do it.

She sat in the lobby and watched as he approached her. He was so handsome still. Did his family age well? Not a question that could really be answered. He was an only child and his parents had both died when he was in his early forties. She had no recollection of them. They had lived in Grafton in northern New South Wales. She had a vague memory of broad streets lined by purple flowering trees if her grandparents were mentioned, no picture in her mind of either of them, just the jacarandas. From what she knew he had been on his own long before their death in any case; studying in Sydney, then London, distancing himself from his country town roots, more by education and sophistication than geography. Had he been able to communicate with them at all in the end? Had he been able to communicate with them ever?

* * *

Frederick stood beside his father at the long workbench. It was nine in the morning and the heat was building, but the dew had not completely evaporated and the pungent fragrance of the large, lemon-scented gum tree just outside the shed wafted through the open door. It would be a searing hot day. They had started early. Maybe they could finish it today before the heat really set in, before the long trip to Sydney tomorrow. They worked in silence; he on the seat, his father on the stand. Each piece so beautifully turned, the rich red of the mahogany gleaming. So many months in the making, and then the countless coats of shellac alternating with pumice, more sanding, more shellac; its smell mingled with the olive oil that let the pad glide across the ever glossier surface. Would this really be the final glaze? Could the thing be done in time? She had wanted it for so long and now she might have it before he left her.

His father's task was infinitely the harder but matched by the difference in their respective experience and skill. The dance of their hands across the wood, the poised pressure of the glide or swirl required to hone the perfection of the polishing, the wordless communication in this place where they could at last find a way to be at peace; this was the best that he would carry with him, the best he had been given of this taciturn man, his father. It was a place where the sadness that plumbed his father's being, and threatened to drag him too into its oblivion, lifted enough to allow proximity. Yet even here they were present: his father's father and older brothers who had gone to war never to return, for this skill and pleasure had been theirs too. His father had stopped believing in God back then as a child, and had had no one to blame or appeal to for his own survival in the Second World War, no one to thank for the son born during that time.

How would his mother feel, seated at last on this fine piano stool they were creating for her, playing the instrument that had brought life into their house, had provided him the means to escape the desperate stillness and grief that pervaded the very air they all breathed together in this place, that up until now had been his home? A scholarship, the Sydney Conservatorium of Music: the dreams she had dreamed for him were to come true. Would she enjoy this parting gift from him, or would it become yet another memento of life's tragedy? He could feel nothing for her ghosts in photo frames, her father, her uncles, all these young men in uniform who had left desolation in the wake of their meaningless death on a distant beach, the awful carnage that had been orchestrated by the arrogance of a British general and then somehow glorified, with the aftermath left to ricochet down the generations all these thousands of miles away. His grandmother, her mother, had clung to him, loved him too fiercely as the living vestige of those she had lost. He could not bear their intensity. He had no choice but to leave.

* * *

Anna longed to stop this preoccupation with her father, yet another attempt to make sense of herself by trying to fathom him. She was his child, she was not him, not her mother, in many ways nothing like either yet somehow a combination of both. Undoubtedly any day or hour he would be gone and she might not see him again for months or even years. What did she want of him? He was just a few steps away.

"Anna, my dear." She rose to greet him and he leant forward to kiss her on the cheek. "I hope I haven't kept you."

"It's fine, Dad. I know I'm early, thanks for coming down. I just wanted to get out of the house."

"Still no Louis?"

She was about to make some evasive, placating comment but stopped herself. "No, Louis has no interest in hospitals or babies. Or, it seems, in me." Her voice quivered slightly. "We're sleeping in separate rooms, he didn't come home last night, and I got out of the house early this morning to avoid running into him."

They were standing side by side in the hotel lobby. Frederick said nothing. He seemed deeply uncomfortable.

"Sorry, Dad. Shall we go through and get breakfast?"

He continued to stand in silence, then reached out and put his hand on top of hers. It was such an unfamiliar gesture that she almost pulled her hand away, but stopped herself before she did so. She hoped he had not noticed.

He patted her hand. "I'm not really in the mood for breakfast. Why don't we walk out and find somewhere for coffee?"

He was staying in a boutique hotel in Flinders Street, on the outer border of the grid that was Melbourne's central business district. The street was not very busy here, away from the railway stations and public transport routes, and the winter air was cold against their faces. They walked uphill in silence in the direction of the Fitzroy Gardens.

"I'm afraid neither your mother nor I are much of an example to you when it comes to successful relationships. It's a wonder to me that you and your sister have done as well as you have."

"I'm amazed that you've given it any thought."

He stopped walking. "You can be cutting!"

She looked at him with genuine surprise. "I'm sorry, Dad. I didn't mean to be, truly. I've just never imagined you considering what life might be like for either Chloe or me. I've always figured that you think of us out of a sense of obligation that comes to mind now and then, or at certain times of year. I don't mean it in a harsh way. For me it's far better than Mum. She only seems to think about what she can get out of relating to either of us; she uses us emotionally in very different ways. I can never see it coming, it's better just to stay away."

They continued walking again, side by side, their pace brisk once more. He glanced her way. "This is a strange conversation."

She looked at the ground in front of her. "It's probably the first real conversation we've had since I was nine."

"That long, Anna?" His voice was both bemused and sad. They walked in silence for some time, their steps more measured, their pace slowing. He spoke again, his voice serious and calm. "I am sorry, so sorry that I didn't make the time to see you last year. I understand now how hard it must have been for you, now that I have been here with Chloe through this. Especially since I've seen Daniel."

He stopped walking and stood still. "Is there any way I can make amends?"

Anna stopped too. She stood staring straight ahead for some moments, then turned to face him. She looked directly into his eyes. "Come with me and visit Anton's grave?"

He met her gaze steadily. "I fly out tomorrow morning."

"Then come with me this afternoon." Both her look and her tone were filled with challenge. She was tired of empty words; this was a moment of opportunity or it was nothing.

Instinctively Frederick understood this. "Yes, I'll come."

They were in the Treasury Gardens. The morning sun shone on the grass which looked strangely emerald green in the intense light. Anna knew she would always associate the colour with this moment.

* * *

Anna climbed out of the taxi and stood staring at the building that loomed above her. Frederick paid the driver and followed her. He took her arm and guided her forward. "Well, shall we?" He smiled at her encouragingly.

"I don't get it, Dad. I just don't understand how you find this bearable! How are you and Mum suddenly okay about seeing each other? All these years of warfare and misery and now you take tea together?"

"We're hardly friendly. There's just nothing there any more; nothing in it, no hold, nothing. She has no meaning for me, no relevance in my life. It was like meeting a stranger. I don't know what else to say about it."

Anna walked beside her father in silence into the hospital. Might she feel that way about Louis one day? She wished she was already there, that she did not have to go through the saga of an ending and separation, or deal with whatever recriminations and nastiness he would inevitably throw her way. She heard his taunting jibe in her head, "There's nothing for you there, that's Chloe's baby." For all their cruelty his words had some relevance. Yet he was wrong. There was so much that had changed in the last few days that related directly to forcing herself through these hospital doors. Could she really imagine a life without him? She felt suddenly strangely enlivened. This visit seemed less foreboding. Her father was coming to say farewell to her sister, but whatever transpired here, he had agreed to leave with her and go to the cemetery afterwards. She thought for a moment of offering to take him to the airport tomorrow, but stopped herself. He did not do airport farewells. He never had.

They could hear voices and conversation from Chloe's room as they approached it. The room seemed to be bursting with solicitous visitors: Adrian, his parents, her mother all hovering. A bassinet stood empty next to the bed, and there in the centre of the room was Chloe with Daniel asleep in her arms. The buzz of conversation was focused on these two: she should put him in the bassinet now, not tire herself, not tire him. Chloe looked amazing, like a figure from a Botticelli: pale and aloof, remote from those surrounding her, yet brimming with femininity and love as she gazed at her baby.

Anna and Frederick stood at the doorway. There seemed no possible way they could fit in the room. Felicity looked up and saw them first. She stared at Frederick, then gave him a small smile and he nodded back in acknowledgement of her. So normal, so breathtakingly normal! Anna was profoundly glad to have come, to have witnessed this interchange, though it passed unnoticed by everyone else in the room. Even should it never occur again in her life, it had been inconceivable just three days ago, and it had happened. Her mother seemed not to see her at all. Anna felt only relief; far better not to be acknowledged than to be asked for something she could never fully fathom, or that she had no chance of being able to fulfil however hard she tried to comply, and infinitely better than being attacked.

"Frederick, Anna, come in, come in. Such a joyous day! Violet and I will have to be on our way shortly. Squeeze in, we're all family here!" Phillip's pleasure was genuine and deep. He was overjoyed to see his grandson where he should be, in his mother's arms and surrounded by family. His relief was palpable. Maybe Adrian's little family would be alright after all, maybe he would not have to face the grief he had been bracing himself for but praying to be saved from.

Chloe looked up and smiled serenely at both her father and Anna. "I told you Annie. I told you, didn't I? I knew God wouldn't let anyone as beautiful as Daniel suffer too long."

Frederick winced and Anna's face clouded with sadness and confusion. Her eyes filled with tears and she stared straight ahead, at a point on the wall beyond her sister, willing herself with everything she had in her not to fall apart, not to cry in front of these people.

"I don't believe it!" Adrian's voice was low but full of venom and fury. "Look at you, dressed all in black, like a crow, like you're wearing a shroud! This is a time of celebration and life. I'm so sick of your grief and tragedy!"

Everyone's eyes turned on Anna. Dressed in a black dress and long grey cardigan with a small pearl pendant at her neck, she looked immensely sad, there was poignancy about her. Daniel whimpered and Chloe looked down, rocking him and cooing to him, trying to soothe him. It was as if she had not heard Adrian, as if Daniel and she were alone in the room and the crowd of family around her had ceased to exist. Felicity looked on with a strange excited smile and Frederick appeared stunned, incapacitated by this unexpected and inexplicable rudeness.

"That's quite enough, Adrian." Phillip's voice was strained.

Violet gently pushed past her husband and placed her arm around Anna's shoulders. She turned her head pointedly away from Adrian and spoke to Anna in a soft clear voice. "I am so sorry, Anna. You lost a baby didn't you, a year ago?"

Anna remembered. Phillip and Violet had sent flowers and a small, blue and white card. They had been kind even then. Only Bill from work and his wife and one of the receptionists had come to the funeral. But Phillip and Violet had sent flowers.

Anna did her best to tolerate the arm about her shoulders, but her own body went rigid in response. She began to feel hot and trapped and attempted to move away from Violet's warm, slim body beside her without seeming to shrug her off, but there was no way it could be done with grace. Violet felt her stiffness, removed her arm and let it hang by her side awkwardly. She was at a loss with these strange people who did not respond in any familiar way to the acts of human kindness that were the staple of her life and informed her sense of being.

"Don't bother, Mum. She's not worth it. None of them are." Adrian glared at Frederick mostly, but then at Anna and strangely at Felicity too.

Violet was frightened by her son's violent emotions and repeated departure from the measured expression of emotion and civility that were expected of him. She felt she must do her best to silence him and restore some sense of order. She looked imploringly at Frederick. "He's been under enormous strain these last few days. I'm sure he doesn't mean a word of this."

Phillip followed her cue. He was deeply ashamed of his son and shocked by his outbursts. "Adrian, why don't you come with your mother and me? Let Chloe's family have some time with Daniel and her."

Adrian scowled. "I am Chloe's family."

Phillip ignored him and turned to Frederick. "You'll be leaving soon I take it?"

"Yes, yes, I fly out tomorrow morning. I'm here to say goodbye."

Felicity let out a sigh and Chloe looked up from her baby, suddenly present to the world once more. "You're leaving, Dad?" Her voice was plaintive.

"I have to, sweetheart. I'm due in Berlin for a performance on Saturday. Even with the time difference I'll be pushing it." He smiled at her. "I'm aging you know, jet lag gets to me these days, never used to." He looked at Phillip and Violet for confirmation of this regrettable fact of life. Their experience of flying amounted to one holiday in New Zealand in their youth, but they nodded in agreement.

Adrian relaxed. He was leaving; this annoying superior charlatan was leaving. That was all that mattered. Let him take centre stage for the moment. It was what he was best at. Chloe would be sad for a while, but she would soon forget him in her preoccupation with Daniel. If Frederick stayed true to form they would hear nothing from him until a card and presents came at Christmas. These would now include Daniel of course. Tokenistic tributes, that was all he was good for. Anna? Why had he lashed out at her like that? She was of no relevance at all. They could head back to Ballarat in a few days. Their life would go back to normal, but with the added blessing of their son to be ever grateful for. It was over. This trial was over.

Adrian extended his hand. "Goodbye, Frederick. Hope you have a good flight to Europe." He would show the old goat up at his own game.

Frederick took the proffered hand and shook it briefly. "Goodbye, Adrian. Take good care of my daughter and grandson."

Adrian's hands were back by his sides. He clenched his fists. Was he being baited? If so he was not going to perform on cue. He could be magnanimous too. "My pleasure, I assure you."

"Glad to hear it." Frederick smiled slightly. He felt a moment of concern for Chloe in her life with this brittle, angry young man. He turned to Phillip and Violet to say his farewells. A great display of leave-taking followed, full of kissing and attempts at affection from Violet and Phillip. Adrian reserved these for his wife and son, while the others in the room struggled with what felt to them like an onslaught of intrusive physicality.

With the departure of the Hargraves the hubbub of life in the room ceased abruptly. A very different atmosphere prevailed; Chloe remained at the centre holding Daniel, as she had been all along, her parents stood on either side of her bed, and Anna was poised strategically near the door: all were still and silent. Anna looked at her parents and sister. When had the four of them last been in the same room together, twenty-five years ago perhaps? Maybe not so long: there had been handovers when they were children, but to be like this, silent in each other's company, however momentarily, when? What she remembered most was the bitter animosity between her parents after their relationship had ended, and their hatred of one another that was hard to separate from how they felt about the children they both shared and who kept them bound to some form of actual relating.

Might her mother have led a very different life if she had had no children to poison in her attempt to wreak vengeance on the husband who rejected her? Oh God, she was at it again, blaming her very existence for this woman's unhappiness. She stared at her mother; observing her at leisure was also such a rarity, made possible because her mother's complete focus was directed at her father. She looked more relaxed and happier than Anna could ever remember seeing her. Many of the lines on her face had softened and she was gazing at Frederick with something akin to adoration. It suddenly felt quite sick, no sickening, and completely unpredictable. Anna wanted to leave. Chloe was cocooned in her bond with Daniel; the Hargraves had been wrong: it was Adrian and they who were her true family now. If only someone would say something, the sham of some kind of normalcy was better than this.

"Can I hold him?" Frederick had approached the bed and was reaching for Daniel. Chloe placed him tenderly in her father's arms, then looked up and beamed at Anna, who worked with everything in herself to believe that this was her sister's wish for validation and not a gesture of triumph. It could be either or both, but she had to believe the first if she was to maintain some love for Chloe. Frederick cradled the little boy with care as he moved to the chair beside the bed and sat down. He gazed at his grandson and smiled. Anna found herself surprised that her father was so adept at handling a baby. Why, she did not know, he was the father of two, but he had always been spoken of by her mother as an absent father. Yet he was a natural with babies.

"You always wanted a boy, didn't you?" Felicity's voice was soft.

He looked up at her. "Perhaps, but not instead of my girls." He turned to Chloe. "I'm so glad to meet Daniel. It's an absolute privilege." He smiled at Daniel and then at Chloe. He looked up at Anna who was shocked to see that his eyes were moist. "I'm just so sorry I never met Anton."

"None of us met Anton. Adrian and I were in Bali on our honeymoon, and you went on a trip to Central Australia, didn't you, Mum?"

"He came early. He wasn't due for more than a month." Felicity sounded uncharacteristically guilty and defensive. Her voice had regained some of its usual harshness. "If that Louis had been here things might have been different."

"You were all alone, Anna? I didn't know." Frederick sounded deeply shocked.

"Pah!" Felicity stood glaring at Frederick as he sat cradling Daniel, his focus completely on Anna. "Don't play the doting father, I won't have it!" She was almost shrieking. "Where were you, Frederick? On the other side of the world! Like that fool of a musician she's with. 'Poor Anna, all alone'." She was mocking him with a sing-song, taunting voice. "Please give it a break. Give us all a break." She started laughing shrilly.

Anna and Chloe looked on blankly, frozen. It was the stuff of their childhood all over again. The bubble of their mother's sudden rekindled infatuation with their father had popped. The jealous, raging banshee-woman was back.

"You're really quite mad, aren't you?" Frederick looked directly at Felicity as though she was some strange species of fish. He said it so calmly; a statement of fact from a disinterested observer.

The sisters sprang to life in unison; Chloe reached for Daniel and Anna moved to her father's side as soon as he stood and handed the baby to Chloe.

"I think it's time we left, Dad."

"It's been so wonderful that you've been here, Dad. Thank you for taking time off, for staying. I can't tell you how much it means to me. Please come back and see us, soon." Chloe's eyes were brimming with tears and she squeezed her father's hand as he leant forward and kissed her farewell.

"Goodbye, sweetheart. I'll do my best." He was about to leave but bent and kissed his sleeping grandson on his head.

Felicity looked around her in confusion. They were all behaving like a loving family and as though she did not exist. Anna and her father were at the door when Frederick turned. "Goodbye, Felicity. I'm very glad that we met again after all these years." He smiled enigmatically at her and walked out.

* * *

"I'm sorry about this, Dad. I should have brought the car. It's such a long taxi ride to the cemetery."

Frederick glanced at her reassuringly. "It's perfectly alright. This is my preferred mode of transport. I enjoy taxi rides; they give me time to think or to look at the city I'm in without the stress of negotiating the traffic and road rules, though there have been a few notable exceptions!" He laughed as if about to share a story with her, but seemed to change his mind. "Of course, I'm most often on my own, and in and out of a city in a hurry."

Anna wondered what he had been about to tell her. "It's the opposite for me. I drive everywhere, literally. I need my car at work and Louis never wants to drive, so I'm the chauffeur. I can't remember when I last took a taxi, and I don't think I've been on public transport, in Australia at least, for more than ten years, before this week that is."

"It has been a most unusual week for all of us." Her father looked at her steadily. "Has your mother always been like this with you?"

* * *

"Anything you have in black and white, Anna; that pinstripe suit and maybe the navy silk dress." Felicity's instructions rang out from the handset on the bed. Louis walked into the bedroom, looked at Anna directly and pulled a quizzical face. She put her finger to her lips as she continued to rummage through her wardrobe. "If you can be here by eleven it will give her a chance to get to the shops if none of them work."

"Okay, Mum, I should be able to make it. See you soon." She turned off the handset and held up the clothes she had taken out of the cupboard; the things her mother had asked for as well as a black straight skirt and white linen blouse.

"Fuck me!" Louis stood at attention and saluted. "You're really going to rush over at Mummy's bidding again?" He moved towards her and pulled her to him playfully. He took the clothes on their hangers from her hand and tossed them on the bed.

"Louis, I can't." She made to push him away but it was a half-hearted attempt and she laughed at him as he nuzzled her neck.

"What's going to happen if you're late? Let me guess, Chloe won't meet your mother's approval as she heads out for some special date?" He sat heavily on the bed, grabbed her hand and pulled her onto the bed beside him.

"Yes, it's someone she met during her last teaching round in Ballarat. It must be serious, she's asked him to her graduation."

"I can't see how she'd fit into your clothes anyway."

"We wear the same size. She's shorter that's all."

"That's not all." He began playing with her hips and bottom.

"Don't begin to go there, Louis. I'm not interested!" She stood up once more and lifted the crushed clothes off the bed. "I said I'd get these there by eleven, I'd better go."

"Honestly, honey, what is it with you girls? Chloe's what, twenty-eight, and still living with Mummy? You jump to whenever she rings?" He made another grab for her hand but let it slide out of his grasp as she moved towards the door. "Okay, but from now on don't put the dragon on speakerphone. I can't stand to hear the way she talks to you."

Anna looked at him strangely for a moment, nodded yes and left the room.

She pulled up in the driveway of her mother's house. She had lived there for at least ten years during her teens and early twenties but it was not a place she could call home. Why was Chloe still living there? Chloe was so much more stable now. She had been sober for at least three years and she seemed to be actually enjoying her teaching course. From all accounts she had managed her country teaching rotation well. Their mother had only gone up to Ballarat to visit her once in the whole eight week period and Chloe had not returned to Melbourne for weekends at all. It was totally unexpected that either of them would behave this way. It was the longest period of separation between the two of them, ever. Maybe Chloe might find some way to leave their mother after all.

Anna rang the front door bell and her mother answered almost instantly; she must have seen her drive in and been waiting. Felicity reached for the clothing, took it from her daughter eagerly and examined each piece in turn. "Good, good. I'm sure she'll look lovely in any of these." She turned and walked away briskly calling out loudly as she went. "Chloe! Chloe!"

Anna followed in her mother's wake as she headed for the lounge room. Chloe wandered into the room in her dressing gown and looking like she had not long been out of bed. "Hi Annie, thanks for bringing these over. Have you had breakfast yet?"

"Don't be ridiculous, Chloe, of course she's had breakfast. The rest of the world moves to a different clock than you do."

Felicity rarely looked either of her daughters in the eye when she spoke to them. She had a habit of speaking instead to some spot in the air next to them or in the middle of their bodies. Anna and Chloe exchanged a look quite unnoticed by their mother; a look of greeting and condolence each with the other. Chloe stood passively and watched as their mother held each piece of clothing in turn in front of her for appraisal.

Finally Felicity spoke. "I think the navy is best."

Chloe looked to Anna. "What do you think, Annie?"

"I think it might work. Why don't you try it on." She suddenly remembered what Louis had said and wished she had not brought so many of her nicest things for Chloe to wear. Mightn't Chloe be better off buying her own dress for a special occasion?

But Chloe was holding the dress against her body and swaying slightly from side to side, watching it move with her. "I don't suppose you brought that lovely blister-pearl pendant of yours with it, did you? It would just be perfect."

Anna spoke before her mother had a chance to give the idea traction. "No, I didn't think of it. I have to get back. We're heading out for lunch soon." She was making it up as she went, but it need not be a lie: she could take Louis out to eat when she got back. She realised she was changing. Once she might well have left and returned with the pendant.

"Adrian is a wonderful young man, Anna. I would not be at all surprised if he proposes to your sister very shortly."

The comment was aimed at Anna, but Chloe became agitated at once. "You mustn't say things like that, Mum. I can't bring him here if you're going to say things like that." She began to pace back and forth. "You'll spoil everything. He's not some-one who rushes into things."

"Oh, alright, Chloe! I won't speak to him at all unless you want me too. I'm just saying that he seems a caring and honourable young man. But it is going to be so strange if you end up in Ballarat, after I did everything I could to leave there." She remembered Anna and turned to her. "You would choose a musician, wouldn't you? Always your father's daughter. Well, now you are reaping the benefits."

Anna on this occasion did grasp that her mother was trying to hurt her, that she assumed it was Louis who was reluctant to marry, perhaps because they had been together for three years and had recently bought a house. It had clearly not occurred to her that Anna might refuse to entertain the idea of marriage for her own reasons. She feigned ignorance. "I'm not the only daughter he has. Isn't he paying for Chloe's degree?"

"As he did for yours!"

"Yes Mum, but I'm grateful."

"I know how he spoils you and Louis, that he gave you money towards your house. He's always been able to buy your love."

Anna looked at Chloe who avoided her eyes. It was the only way their mother could have found out. Anna turned away from her mother and sister and walked to the door. "No Mum, he's always had my love."

* * *

Anna felt nervous at the very thought of answering her father's question, but the small talk could not last. "It's worse since I've been with Louis. She and Louis dislike each other and I just haven't run around after her or Chloe any more. I have my own life and she can't stand it."

119

"It seems to me that we all owe you the greatest of apologies. Your mother did seem guilty about being out of Melbourne when Anton was born."

"That's not the way it was, Dad. She was in Melbourne, not Central Australia, that's just the version of the story she told Chloe. She was furious with me because I didn't ring her until after Anton died."

Anna's body felt suddenly very heavy, weighted down with the memory and the pain of that time. Her skin went pale, her breathing slowed, and her voice softened to the point where Frederick had to listen very acutely to hear what she was saying. "He was so sick, it all happened so fast. I was desperately trying to reach Louis, but he was in the middle of some music negotiations in LA and had his phone switched off. I finally tracked him down through Charlie, his manager. It was all so awful ..." She was looking down at her hands. "Mum flew to Alice Springs the day before Anton's funeral."

"I'm so sorry that she is your mother. That she was who I chose."

"That's absurd Dad! If you hadn't I wouldn't be here, it wouldn't be me you'd be having this conversation with. I've wished she was different for so long, but I'm finally done with trying to second-guess her. I just don't care any more." She leant forward and looked out of the window. She spoke to the taxi driver. "The main entrance please, and up to the florist." She turned back to her father. "We're almost there." She felt intensely anxious, for she feared he would be overwhelmed by what she was asking of him and would retreat from her. They had come so far.

* * *

They stood at the edge of the Children's Lawn and looked out onto a green sea awash with fluttering rainbow-coloured windmills and bright flowers. Anna clutched her bunch of bright yellow and white daises to her chest with one hand, while she held a small plastic vase that she had collected from a wire cage filled with vases in the other.

"It's such a cheerful looking place." Frederick felt a sudden sense of dread, but he held his arm out to his daughter and she laced hers through it, leaning on him slightly as they stepped onto the lawn. They walked on steadily, Anna weaving her way through the rows of memorial plaques, many with flowers in the vases beside them, and almost all of them with treasured collections; a little family of plaster bears, a small cluster of reclining angels, a gathering of fairies, a special pony, some cars, a red dinosaur.

Frederick's eyes filled with tears, while Anna walked on, a sense of purpose and urgency about her. She was afraid she had got it wrong, that somehow she would not be able to find his grave. She looked back towards the avenue where the taxi was waiting. She noted the position of the fountain: a little naked cherub playing two long fluted reeds, from one of which the water flowed down and fell away. She orientated herself, stopped and took a deep breath, then smiled suddenly. "This is right, it's just over here." She stopped in front of a grave-stone and stared at it. She let go of her father's arm and knelt down placing her flowers on the ground beside her. She began to brush away the grass and twigs that had fallen on the grave in a purposeful and yet distracted, even dreamlike, way. The gentle motion of her hand seemed to caress the little plaque. Frederick could only see her in profile. He felt a wave of sadness unlike any he could remember feeling. His vision was blurred and he felt slightly off balance. She lifted the vase. "I'll just take this over to the tap. I need to fill it up."

She did not look at him directly and smiled at a spot to the right of him as she got to her feet slowly and walked away. He looked down at the grave with its small square plaque. "In loving memory of Anton Edward Mason-Williams …"

So Daniel and Anton both carried his middle name. Did Chloe even realise? He felt a deep searing pain in his chest, like he had been winded but worse. Beads of perspiration clung to his face. He fumbled in his trouser pocket and pulled out a small tin, flicked it open, and placed one of the tiny tablets in it under his tongue, then shoved it back into his pocket before she returned. He crouched before the grave. He had never passed out in his life and did not want the indignity of doing so, more than anything not here or now, not in front of Anna.

He sensed her presence next to him as she crouched beside him. She placed the little vase back on top of the grave before turning to look at him. He felt her hand on his shoulder. "Dad, are you okay? You look quite grey." She touched his forehead. His skin was cold and clammy. Her hand went to his wrist to take his pulse in the reflex action of a doctor with someone who was clearly unwell. "Are you in pain? Can you stand up? I'll help you to the bench over there." She went pale too. "I'm so sorry if this is too much for you. I shouldn't have insisted you come."

The pain began to ease and he spoke to her in a soft vulnerable voice, so different from his usual confidence and aplomb. "I think I'll be okay, Annie. Yes, let's go over to that bench."

Anna helped him up and took his arm, guiding him towards the wooden seat. A woman twenty metres away looked up at them with concern from where she knelt beside a grave, then looked away again not wanting to intrude on their grief. Frederick eased himself onto the seat and Anna sat beside him. "I can see you're in pain, Dad. Have you ever had anything like this before? What's happening right now? You need to tell me."

Frederick braced his body, his arms outstretched on either knee. He had had no intention of letting anyone know, but he could see now it was inevitable that Anna should. "I have a stent in one of the major arteries to my heart." He continued rapidly before his daughter could pummel him with any more questions. "And don't ask me which one because I have no head for that sort of detail. I'm due for bypass surgery next month. I was hoping to put it off, but I suppose that might be folly."

Anna turned to look at him then turned away to stare across the sea of graves. She felt strangely calm. "Don't put it off, Dad, I'd like to see you this Christmas. Remember, we have plans."

He laughed softly. "We do, don't we? Why don't you go and put those flowers on your little boy's grave." His voice trembled ever so slightly as he said the words. "I'll watch from here."

Her eyes met his with gratitude and asked if he really meant it.

"Go on, I'll be fine."

She stood and walked slowly back to the grave. He watched as she pulled the leaves off the stalks and arranged the flowers one by one in the vase, adjusting each to give just the right composition; it was an act of love.

He had not gone to Grafton for his parents' funerals, even though he and Felicity and Anna were based in Melbourne at the time. He had never thought to visit their graves. He had not wanted to return for Anton's funeral. He had been sure that Anna would be accompanied by Louis, surrounded by friends, burdened by her mother's presence. He had told himself that he did not want to add to her distress by some unwelcome confrontation with Felicity, but had that merely been an excuse? In truth he saw now that he had not wanted to be here in this place. Had he been a coward? He looked again at his daughter. He knew that his presence here today was somehow vital to her and yet in two days' time he would be in Berlin and would be completely absorbed in his work, and the music, the orchestra of the day; she would melt into a distant shadow, ever near his heart but not his consciousness. She was right to challenge him; she, Chloe, Daniel, Anton, they would all fade from his mind.

Anna knelt by her son's grave and imagined him in her arms, a reality she had never known in his brief life outside her body. The battle to save him had consumed that time, and she had only been able to hold him in death. They had encouraged her to do it then, told her it would help. Perhaps it had, for otherwise she would never have known the feeling of cradling his small body so close to hers. Tears streamed down her face as they always did in this place, which up until today she had visited rarely and on her own. She remembered him finally in the way she had known him best; his playful movements inside her, the feel of his head or his foot through her belly, her discussions with him when she was alone about how much she longed to see him and all the things she planned to do with him, the songs she would sing in the hope that he would hear her. Louis had been a part of her daydreams; she and Louis and Anton as a family, Louis successful and happy in his work, an American record deal. She had let herself have it all.

She remembered her father suddenly and turned to see him watching her intently. His colour looked far better and he smiled at her and waved in reassurance. She had stopped crying and she smiled back at him. She stood and looked down at the colourful flowers with their happy faces: they would keep him company. It made no sense to think this way from the point of view of the adult atheist in her, but it made perfect sense from some other primitive and superstitious place; it satisfied something, a desire to feel that she was not leaving him all alone in the ground every time she tore herself away. She turned and walked slowly to sit by her father. They sat in silence together for a long time.

Finally she spoke. "Thanks, Dad. I'll always remember this day. Always." She looked at him. "How are you feeling now?"

"I'm fine, I'm fine." He sighed deeply. "So it's confirmed, you'll come to me this Christmas?"

"Yes, I'll come, but not with Louis. I don't see how he and I can last till then." Her voice became more confident. "The truth is I don't think that I love him any more. We haven't got what I want in a relationship, in life."

"Of course, I like Louis, I always have … but Annie, a life alone is far better than a life of misery."

She was silent for a while. When she spoke there was a quiet surety in her voice. "I'm hoping for more than that. There is someone else."

Frederick hesitated. He straightened his body slightly. "Well, he's very welcome at Rhode Island for Christmas."

"Thanks, Dad. I'll let you know. I may come alone or there might even be three of us—he has a daughter."

Her father sighed and gave a soft laugh. "Bring a whole troupe for all I care! Just come Annie."

She summoned her courage. "Can I drive you to the airport tomorrow?'

He did not speak for some time. He turned to look at her but she was staring straight ahead. He did the same. "Thank you for offering, but I think it's best if I get there on my own … My plane leaves at six a.m. and I'll have to be there a couple of hours ahead of time. I'm never a pretty sight at that time in the morning!" He laughed lightly.

SEVEN

She woke confused. Where was she? She felt the containing confines of the single bed with blankets tucked tightly around her and a summer doona on top. The guest room, she was in the guest room, as she had been for the past three nights. It must be Friday morning. She picked up her mobile phone from the bedside table and checked the time; six-thirty, her father would be on his flight to Europe. Bypass surgery next month: she would have to get in touch with him, follow it up, make sure he did not try to delay it, speak with his doctors if he let her. What daydream was she in? Why would he let her? They had never had that kind of relationship. The closeness she had experienced with him in the last few days was real, but any follow-up on her part, other than responding to his invitation to participate in his life again at Christmas, was likely to be seen as an intrusion. She had tried it in her teens. It was so disorienting to grapple with the reality that he was gone.

She pushed herself up in the bed and ruffled her hair. Was it easier to think about her father than to face opening the door and walking into the corridor of her own home? The realisation dawned: she had not seen or spoken with Louis since Tuesday night when his vicious remarks to her in front of Charlie had sundered something. She had been coming home late and leaving early ever since. She had eaten out and gone to a movie on her own the night before just to avoid him, but, as she turned her mind to him fully for the first time in days, it occurred to her that she had no idea when or if he had been home. She felt deeply shocked. She knew that neither of them had called or sent a text message but she also realised that she had not looked for evidence of his presence in the house, only for his absence. It was the opposite of her usual way of being with him: waiting for him, anticipating his moods or reacting to them, thinking of how best to engage or placate him.

She could avoid thinking about any of this further. She could get up, get dressed, and go into work. It was what she had done all through the last year. They were not expecting her back until Monday, but she knew she would be fully booked in no time if she decided to go in. She climbed out of bed and dressed in the clothes she had worn the day before. She opened the door and walked silently down the corridor to the door of their bedroom which was shut. She turned the doorknob tentatively and peered into the darkened room. Her eyes took a few moments to adjust enough so that she could make out that the bed was unmade but empty. He had slept here at some time in the last couple of days but not last night. She felt a strange mix of relief and dread. It would be so easy to avoid a confrontation, to go to work, and wait until they were next in the house together, to find some way to pretend that none of what had transpired this week was real. She felt the pull of it. It was so strong, so familiar.

She walked into the kitchen and turned on the light. The room was clean, unused. Had she tidied it each morning before she left? She had not the slightest recollection of doing so, but it was possible she had done it on automatic. After Anton's death she had done virtually everything on automatic for weeks or even months. She walked into the laundry, opened the back door, and stepped out into their back garden for the first time in days. It was still dark and the sensor lights came on, throwing bright beams and the edgy shadows of trees and bushes across the small back lawn. She made her way to the side of the house. The rubbish bins were half full and had not been put out this week. The recyclables bin had a few wine bottles and twice as many beer bottles in it. He could not have been home much, especially if he and Charlie had polished off most of that together on Tuesday night, which was likely.

She turned and walked to her back door. She hesitated on the step, then pushed open the fly-wire and wooden doors and entered the kitchen. She filled the kettle, switched it on, and stood with her back to it and the bench on which it rested as she surveyed the room. Something had changed. It was so strange to view things this way, to see her home with a dispassionate eye. She realised that she already knew which things she would take with her and which she would leave behind for Louis. It was as if deep down she had kept some inner tally of what each had brought to the relationship, which of the things they had bought together had importance to her, and which she could readily leave behind.

It was eerie to recognise that in her mind this house belonged with Louis, as their farm at Bemm River had always been hers. She would fight him if need be, but she doubted it would come to that. It seemed as if something in her had been preparing for the end of their relationship for a long time, without her consciously being aware of it. She was sure that there had been a window of opportunity for a different life for them, more secure and committed, especially during her pregnancy with Anton, but it had died with him. She was shocked to realise that today the thought of ever conceiving a child again with Louis deeply repulsed her, yet only a few days ago and for the past six months she had been trying to force him to do precisely that.

She walked back to their bedroom. Louis was rarely an early riser, so wherever he was she would have at least a couple of hours to herself before he might come back here. She undressed slowly, savouring something so familiar, done countless previous times in this room, but perhaps being done for the last time now. She tossed her clothes on the bed and reached for her dressing gown that was still hanging on the back of the bedroom door. She put it on and headed for the bathroom, stopping to get a clean towel from the linen cupboard on the way. She turned on the shower, climbed into the large enamelled bath and into the wonderful warmth of the water that streamed down on her from the shower head above. She closed her eyes and let the water course over her head and face, then down her body. She shampooed and conditioned her hair and soaped her body. She felt the tension leave the muscles of her neck and back. She lost herself in the soothing sensuality of it.

"For fuck's sake! If only sex were that good!"

She opened her eyes and was startled to see him standing fully clothed staring at her. "Get out, Louis! Get out now!"

He turned and left the room. She felt violated, both by his presence and his aggression. She had no stomach for either. She turned off the water and dried her hair and body hurriedly. She pulled her dressing gown around her and swept her hair up in the towel. She realised she would have to confront him. Her clothes were all in their bedroom. She looked at herself in the mirror and was stunned by what she saw. She looked so much more alive; her colour was better, her face more relaxed than it had been for a year. She looked strangely well with her hair in a turban, clad in a faded, woollen dressing gown and with Louis loose in the house.

She could not bear the thought of being trapped with him in the bedroom so she turned in the opposite direction and made for the kitchen, but he was there, seated at the table, both his hands clasped before him, resting on it. His head was down, his gaze fixed low, studying his hands intently. She stood in the doorway. He looked up at her. She noted the greyness of his skin, the peppered stubble on his face at least two days in the making, the hurt and anger in his eyes. There was no avoiding this any longer.

"It's time, Louis. Time we talk. Don't you think?" Her tone was strangely calm, neutral. It surprised both of them.

"Don't you want to know where I've been?" He sneered when she did not answer immediately. "Who I've been with?"

"Really?" The word had ice in it, but her voice remained calm. "That might simply make things easier." She looked at him steadily and his bluster lessened. She went on tersely. "Sure we can talk about that, but I'd rather talk about Anton."

"What is there to say? He died." He shuffled in his seat and glared at her and she suddenly became aware of the smell of alcohol mixed with stale perfume that emanated from him when he moved. She felt her stomach churn with disgust.

"I know you think I'm heartless, Anna. No, more likely useless, probably both. But he was alive for one day, just one day."

"No, Louis. He was alive for eight months before that, inside me. You felt him kick and move. We wanted him together. Why didn't you come back? Even in time for his funeral?"

He lifted his head and looked at her directly. "You really want to know?"

She nodded wordlessly.

"You met him, I never did … I didn't come back for his funeral because I felt like killing you … Don't look at me like that, as if I'm some madman. If you hadn't run around after your patients all the time, always covering for that dipshit Don, seeing patients with hepatitis for Christ's sake! Who knows what did it? You might have saved our baby. Our baby! My son!"

"Anton, his name is Anton."

"You named him that."

A year of silence that at last made sense; it was not his grief, it was punishment. She felt strangely calm. "You went overseas during the last six weeks of my pregnancy, and it's my fault that I was overworked and Anton was born prematurely?"

"You see, here we have it. Your mother is with us as we speak."

"Sure, Louis. I'm probably channelling her. I don't give a damn about that any more." She pulled herself away from the doorpost she had been leaning on. "Babies come early for no apparent reason. Did that ever occur to you?" She stood up straight and glared down at him, a quiet rage welling in her. "I'm not Stella! I had your baby. Tragically, for all three of us, he died."

"Yah, Charlie was tied in knots the other night. Thought he'd caused more trouble between us." He laughed mockingly. "Guess he has no idea how far gone we are."

"Maybe neither of us has wanted to admit that until now. Who is she, Louis?"

His face screwed up in pain. "There is no 'she'. I've had a few one night stands, that's all."

"Including last night?"

"Yah, sure."

"Always easy I guess when you're Louis Williams."

"Always easy anyway, sweetheart. Plenty of lonely hearts out there in the real world."

His hands went to his face, covering it, then rubbing at it strangely. He started to sob, making long gasping sounds. He reached towards her; his left arm and hand extended across the table. "Don't stand there like that, Annie. Come over here. Sit with me. We can work this out, baby. I know we can work this out."

She felt a shiver inside her. She moved quietly and sat down opposite him. She placed her hands on her lap and looked at him steadily across the table. "If you really believe that, Louis, you don't know me at all."

His sobs ceased and he looked up at her dry-eyed. "The guy in the Merc?"

"Sure … We've both been looking. The difference is I would never hop into bed with anyone until we're over."

"Semantics, pedantics, Annie, kid yourself if you want to."

"If you say so." She'd had enough of him. "You look like you need a shower and some sleep. I'll get what I need from the bedroom and it's yours." Her tone was perfunctory.

He looked at her sheepishly. "What's happened with Fred? Is he still in town?"

"No, he's on a plane to Europe."

"Is the kid okay?"

"Yes, this grandson survived and he got to see and hold him. I'm sure he's glad he stayed."

"This grandson! Your nephew, sweetheart, no attachment there?"

"Give it a rest, Louis. You missed it. If you'd come to the hospital with me who knows where we'd be now. But you didn't and I met someone else there."

"You're forgetting my sins aren't you, honey? Would my coming to the hospital have made up for those?"

"No, you're right of course, I stand corrected." She could see that he wanted to hurt her, to have the upper hand, to be the one doing the rejecting. She felt so angry. She suddenly hated his terms of endearment that she had always found so compelling: they echoed with emptiness now. She hated him for betraying her, for not having what she needed. She wanted to hurt him back. "Truth is I haven't seen Matthew for a long time, but we were lovers in our teens."

"How wonderful for you! I'm sure you're both eager to take up where you left off. I won't get in your way, Anna. I think we've both had a gut-full, haven't we?"

* * *

Anna focused intently on the screen of her laptop that was open in front of her on the kitchen table. She scrolled through the pages of properties for rent on Realestate.com. She scribbled down the addresses of two that interested her and were open for inspection the next day; a flat in Elsternwick and a town-house in Brighton. She heard her mobile phone ring softly somewhere in the house and then stop. She looked up from the screen and was surprised to find that the room was dark. The blinds were all up and it was dark outside as well. She had been at this much longer than she had thought. Louis had left by mid-morning and she had spent much of the day moving more of her things into the spare room. They had made no agreement. She had no idea when he might return but half suspected he might stay at Charlie's for the time being. Maybe she just wished he would.

She stood and stretched, then turned on the light in the kitchen and closed the blinds before going in search of her phone. She did the same in each room as she progressed through the house. She heard her phone ring again and headed for the spare bedroom. She got to it just after it had ceased ringing. She checked; a private number both times and a message from the last call. She dialled her message bank and listened.

"Hello, Dr Mason, this is Dr Lim from the emergency department at Singapore General Hospital. I'm calling to inform you that your father Mr Frederick Mason was taken off his plane at Singapore Airport this afternoon and is currently having investigations for a suspected cardiac ischaemic event. He asked that you be contacted as his next of kin. You can call back on …" The voice was formal and polite with a Chinese accent and quite devoid of emotion.

She sat on the bed and looked at the phone in her hand blankly. She had an urge to drop it and crawl under the covers of the bed. Instead she stood up and forced herself to walk back to the kitchen, clutching the phone. She sat at the table, pushed aside her laptop, picked up the pen and pulled the pad that lay on the table to her. She absent-mindedly drew a line under the addresses and times written on it as she redialled her voice-mail. She listened to the message once more and wrote down the number to call, then replayed the message again to ensure she had done so correctly. She sat staring at the number written in large bold numbers twice the size of the writing above the line. She felt light-headed and slightly nauseated. She knew that she did not want to make the call, but she also realised that she had to.

She pulled her laptop back and looked up the international dialling codes for Singapore. She dialled and listened with a slow pit of fear grinding just below her sternum. The phone chimed out the international signal and began to ring with long slow beeps.

"Hello, Singapore General Hospital, how can I help you?" A polite female voice, perfect English, only the slight sing-song-like lilt and intonation indicated that its owner might be Asian.

Not the direct number she had hoped for. "Hello, this is Dr Anna Mason ringing from Melbourne, Australia. My father, Frederick Mason, has been taken to your hospital today. I'm returning a call from Dr Lim in the emergency department. Could I speak with him please?"

"Hold the line please, Dr Mason. I will see if I can connect you."

She listened to the recorded music on the phone, and noticed that her hand, with the pen still in it, was trembling slightly. She put the pen down. The wait seemed interminable.

"Putting you through now."

"Hello, Dr Lim?"

A woman's voice answered. "I'm sorry, Dr Mason, but Dr Lim is busy right now. You can talk to your father if you like?"

She felt quite shocked and then relieved. He must be reasonably alright if she could speak to him. "Yes, yes, thank you."

Silence followed and she was not sure if she had lost her connection, although there had been none of the right beeps to indicate that she had. She waited and was considering whether she should hang up and begin the whole process again when the same woman's voice returned.

"Hello, Dr Mason, I have your father here."

She heard the sound of something familiar, was it a suction machine, or perhaps an oxygen pump, as the phone was handed over.

"Anna?" His voice was very clear. He might have still been in the same city.

"Hi Dad, how are you? Have they told you what they think is going on?"

"I was just a bit off colour on the plane. The steward noticed and well … seemed like the safest thing to do, to check it out properly."

She realised he was playing it down. He must have been very unwell for someone to notice. After what had happened at the cemetery the day before, how had she just let him go? Why had she not insisted he be checked medically before he left Australia? She struggled with deep feelings of guilt and regret. "I'll book a flight, Dad. I'm sure I can be there by tomorrow night."

"Don't, Anna. I'm sorry they contacted you and worried you like this."

"You gave my name as next of kin?"

"I always give your name as next of kin."

She felt deeply shocked. "I had no idea."

He laughed. "Fortunately there's been no need for you to know till now … Things seem to be settling here. My plan is to cancel Berlin and fly straight home when they say I'm fit to."

"You don't need someone there in the meantime?"

"Listen, Anna, I'm sure this is all just a precaution, you know how particular they are about everything in Singapore. You can talk to the doctors here when they're free. I'll see if they can call you back."

She felt reassured. He was always so persuasive, she might get the call. "Okay, I'll ring back tomorrow if I don't hear, and I'll let Chloe know."

"Please don't involve your sister in this. She's just recovering from the fear that her son might die, she really doesn't need to worry about her old father."

"I don't think she'd forgive me if anything happened to you and she found out I knew you were in hospital and didn't tell her." Her tone was matter of fact.

"I see I've created a monster. From what I understand I'll probably be fit to fly in a couple of days."

She knew it was his default position; optimism unless proven otherwise. She was not going to challenge it at such a time. His ECG results would already be known and his early cardiac enzyme levels might be in, but he would have to wait for further results before being cleared to fly, that much was certain.

"Tell your doctor it's okay to ring at any time, Dad. It doesn't matter about the time difference. I'll keep my phone by my bed."

* * *

The call came at ten the next morning. She was in the kitchen eating cereal. Strangely, she had slept through the night.

"Hello?"

"Hello, Dr Mason?"

"Yes."

"This is Dr Lim from Singapore General. Yes, so your father wanted me to let you know his results. His test results confirm a small recent anterior infarct. He is stable at the moment and pain free. He has no sign of cardiac failure. As you know these are all favourable indicators for him. We are planning to keep him in hospital for a few more days at least. He should be fit to fly after two weeks, if everything is stable. We strongly recommend that he sees his cardiologist on returning to America."

"Dr Lim, would it help if I came to Singapore and got a hotel room where he can recover after his discharge, until he's well enough to fly?"

"That would be very sensible, Dr Mason. I know your father is a most successful man and wise I am sure, but I think to have you here could be of great benefit to him. He does not seem to understand that the consequences could be serious for him, that he is at risk." He was direct and earnest.

Anna appreciated both. She made a mental note to talk to her father about going ahead with his surgery when he got back to the States. She felt validated; if he could put her down as next of kin then she might after all have the right to advocate for optimal treatment with him. She felt strong enough at least to take the risk.

"Thank you for getting back to me, Dr Lim. Is my father still in the emergency department? Can I call him there?"

"He has been admitted to the Coronary Care Unit. I can try and have this call transferred."

"Please don't worry. I'll call the hospital back directly. Thank you so much for calling, and for all you have done."

She caught her breath and dialled, then waited nervously until the call was put through. Would he allow it?

"Hello?"

"Hi Dad, it's Anna."

"Hi Anna, this is something of a shock for me. It's good to hear your voice."

"I'm so sorry, Dad. I should have taken you in for a check-up as soon as we left the cemetery on Thursday. I don't know what happened to me. I want to come over when they let you out. Get a suite or an apartment." She heard him sigh on the other end of the line and continued hurriedly. "I promise I won't crowd you. I'll play secretary, ring your doctors in the States, liaise with your PA, whatever you need, then get out of your way." She laughed strangely. "I'll go see the sights."

Frederick heard how afraid she was that something would happen to him, but maybe even more so that he would say no; that he would reject her and allow her no opportunity to see him again. He had a sudden wave of recognition of his own mortality. Christmas was six months away. Who knew how the treatment ahead of him would go. "On one condition."

"Anything."

"You let me pay for your flights, for the accommodation, for anything it costs you to miss your work."

Anna sighed softly with relief. He was going to let her come. "Whatever works for you, Dad, we can sort that out later."

She sat in silence after ending the call, then suddenly came to and checked her watch. There were still forty-five minutes before the first of the two properties she wanted to inspect was open and it was only ten minutes' drive away. She looked at her mobile phone sitting on the table. Her father had been against it, but surely Chloe had a right to know. What if something else happened to him? She sat on the bed, picked up her phone, and rang Chloe's mobile number. It rang out. There was no message or voicemail. What was she thinking? Most likely Chloe had not taken her phone to hospital and it was lying somewhere out of charge. Adrian would be easy to contact but she could not bear the thought of ringing him. Anna rang the hospital and asked for Chloe's room. The phone was answered immediately. "Hello, Adrian Hargraves speaking." He was whispering.

It seemed that a verbal encounter with him was unavoidable. Anna summoned all her resolve. "Hello Adrian. Can I speak to Chloe?"

"Chloe's sleeping. I don't want to disturb her."

So, he was going to play gatekeeper. "Can you tell her I called when she wakes up?" She tried to keep her tone neutral but did not succeed, her voice had an edge. She regretted it. He was likely to retaliate and not tell Chloe. He might do so out of bloody-mindedness in any case. "It's important, Adrian. It's about Dad." It seemed somehow disloyal to her father to let him know any more than that.

Adrian made an odd dismissive sound. "Of course it's important if it's about your father." His voice was a quiet hiss laced with contempt.

She felt so tired of him, small, small man that he was. She could not bear to explain herself to him. His vile behaviour of the last week resounded in her. He had been under enormous strain, surely, but had he ever been anything other than offensive, or at best offhand, in the time she had known him? No memory of any behaviour that had approximated to common courtesy surfaced to swing the scales in his favour. She pressed the "end call" button on her phone without replying. She felt unsettled by the call, but she had tried. If she did not hear back from Chloe she might call again. Maybe it would be best to ring once she got to Singapore and saw how her father actually was. She sat forward. She really ought to go if she wanted to get to the apartment in time to see it. She picked up her phone again and rapidly searched a number. She looked at it intently then dialled.

He answered at once. "Hello?"

"Hi Matthew, it's me. Are you working today? Do you have Rose with you?" She was surprised to hear her voice falter.

"What is it, Anna, what's happened?"

She laughed, trying to make light of it, not wanting to need him; yet knowing that she did. "I'm leaving Louis. My father's had a heart attack. He's in hospital in Singapore. I'm planning to fly there sometime next week. I'm just about to inspect a flat in Elsternwick that sounds good and has a six month lease." She stopped talking, looked at her watch and sighed. "And I've actually got to get in the car right now to be there in time. This is all intense and messy I know, but I'd really like to see you. Are you free, can you meet me at St Kilda pier in an hour?"

"Go look at the flat, Anna. I'm free. I'll see you in an hour."

* * *

It was a grey day and the wind was icy. The long pier that stretched before her was gay despite the dullness of the day. The lines of white posts on the left side of its wide boardwalk

139

formed a contrast to the threatening skies. She kept by the posts as she made for the elegant kiosk with its Federation style symmetry and cast iron roof. There was hardly anyone on the pier: an old man walking a small black and tan spaniel, a couple heading for the beach pushing a pram who hurried past her as she headed out towards Matthew. She had seen him at once, leaning against the railings to the left of the kiosk. Dressed in blue jeans and a navy seaman's jacket he looked more familiar, easier to recognise as the young man she had known, grown to full manhood. She watched him get larger. She knew instinctively that she would be able to depend on him, if that was what he decided to offer her. It was the most startling thing about him. He was the kind of man neither Louis nor her father could ever be. He was gazing at her intently as she approached him.

Anna hurried her pace and almost ran the last few metres to reach him. He pulled away from the railing and stood facing her. She was flushed with the exertion of the walk but there was something else as well: she looked different, her face was more open, happier than he could ever remember seeing it.

She smiled; an eager, awkward smile. "Thanks for coming."

He reached out and stroked her face. "You're leaving Louis?"

"Yes, that's the plan." She turned her body and stood alongside him. She leant back on the railing and watched the brightly painted little yachts bobbing against their moorings, buffeted about by the rising wind. "I just saw a great little apartment. I've got the application papers in my car." She glanced up at him. "Do you think this is all crazy? Deciding to leave someone one day and considering taking the first apartment you see the next?"

"So acting on impulse isn't your thing?" He was straight-faced but his voice held a strange mixture of tension, humour, and hope.

"Quite out of character." She glanced his way. "Though I have always done it around you, haven't I?" She pulled away from the railing and stood facing him again. "I think I left Louis after Anton died, or he left me. I just couldn't face the fact, neither of us could." She looked at him with a mixture of respect and gratitude. It was such a relief to speak freely.

"Have you told him as yet?"

"Not directly, but I will."

He placed a hand on each of her shoulders. "Rose is with her mother this weekend. What about lunch and a walk on the beach or dinner tonight?"

"What about both?" She hugged him and buried her head in his chest.

They bought fish and chips at the kiosk and set out across the beach; a long slow walk, following the lines of palm trees that tracked along Beaconsfield Parade, ploughing through the soft sand at first then leaving it to walk along the firmness of the water's edge. They dodged the dead jellyfish and clumps of seaweed thrown up by the tide. They were oblivious to the people they passed; those walking dogs, those just braving the cold and wind. They barely gave the kitesurfers a look. They stopped on a concrete jetty and threw their remaining food to the circling gulls, who fought for it. They turned and headed back. They walked in silence most of the time, not touching but taking great pleasure in the other's nearness.

Matthew stopped suddenly as they neared St Kilda pier. "Where are you parked?"

She pointed. "A few hundred metres up the road."

"I'm just here. Why don't I give you a lift to your car, or better still, you could follow me back to my place?" He laughed; a soft eager laugh.

"Hadn't I better go home and get changed for dinner?"

"There's a long time before dinner. Come back to my place for a while, we can see what we feel like later." He wanted her, but even more so he felt that he needed to claim her: he did not want to risk her returning to Louis. This was such a fragile time, anything was possible. He stood very close to her and ran his hand under the back of her hair, playing with it.

She felt a deep sense of warmth and pleasure at his touch. He leaned over and kissed her gently at first, then more deeply. She kissed him back. It was so amazing to kiss him passionately, without having to block out the bitter taste of alcohol as she always had to with Louis. Louis, she felt like she was being unfaithful to him just kissing someone else. Why, if it was over between them, when he had betrayed her? It was going to take time to adjust.

Matthew waited for her to pull up behind his car, opened her door for her, and extended his hand to help her from the car. He wrapped his arm around her shoulders as they walked through the garden towards the front porch. She stopped at the daphne bush and picked a sprig of the tiny white and pink flowers. She held them first to her nose to drink in their heady aroma, then to his so he could do the same. It was only mid-afternoon but the gloominess of the day made it look much later. He walked ahead of her up the stairs but she held on lightly to the hand he trailed behind him, needing the warmth of his touch to give her the assurance to follow. He unlocked the door and walked in first, turning on the lights as he went. She stood hesitant at the open door.

He reached for her hand and pulled her to him. He leant back against the wall and kicked the door shut. He ran his hands up under her jumper fondling her breasts, then lifting her skirt and feeling the firmness of her bottom and thighs. He ached for her. He stood up and lifted her easily onto him. She straddled his hips, loving the strength and power in his body as he walked with her into the lounge room, gently spilled her onto the couch, and began to undress her, kissing her body, touching her between her legs to caress her, undressing himself as well as he went. She reached up to help him get out of his shirt and jeans. She pulled him on top of her and pressed her hands hard against the tautness of his arms. She ran her fingers over the smoothness of the skin of his shoulders and back. She held his buttocks tightly as he thrust against her and kissed her neck and breasts.

He pulled away from her gently and reached down to his jacket on the ground. He searched in the pockets and found his wallet. He flipped it open, pulled out a condom packet, and tore it open. She reached forward and took it from its packet and held it in one hand then played with his penis with the other.

"Hey Anna, hey that's wonderful but you'd better stop. I want to come inside you."

She laughed and rolled the condom onto his penis. She felt him enter her and begin thrusting deep inside her. Her body moved so easily with his. She felt deep waves of pleasure hit her with each thrust, move from somewhere deep inside her up through her entire body until she felt on the verge of something almost unbearable. She responded to his gentle moans and sighs of pleasure with her own and they too built in intensity. Then it came, a deep sense of release that seeped through her and left her replete and tingling. He must have come at the same time. He was lying on top of her completely relaxed. He kissed her neck and rolled easily onto the ground beside the couch. He laughed loudly. "Well that was worth the wait."

She looked directly into his eyes and laughed with him. He was right.

* * *

Anna looked at her house. The lights were on. She walked determinedly to the front door and turned the key. The house was warm and smelt of food. Louis stood in the hallway in front of her. His face had that soft yearning expression she had not seen for so long, had never thought to see turned her way again.

"I bought Indian for dinner. There's enough for both of us."

"Thanks, but I just came back to freshen up and change. I've got other plans."

He moved closer to her, his expression contrite, pleading. He reached to stroke the side of her face and neck. She felt her whole body tense in response. She pulled away slightly, but enough so that he dropped his hand. He touched her fingers, slipped his hand in hers, and made to lead her to the kitchen.

"No, Louis." She grasped his hand firmly and led him into their lounge room. She let go of his hand and turned on the light. She realised it was probably months since they had spent any time in this room together. Listening to music, watching television, talking, relaxing, the comfortable companionship of life had eluded them. She took his hand once more and led him to the couch. She sat in the armchair just next to it.

"I got a call from Singapore yesterday. Dad's in hospital. He's had a heart attack. I'm planning to go there when he gets out of coronary care. I'll stay with him till he's well enough to fly to the States."

He looked genuinely shocked and concerned. "Of course, baby. I'll come with you. No question."

She stared at him in surprise. "What about your tour?"

"It's not till next month." He saw her look of distrust. He leant forward and took her hand. "You come first, baby. We can get through this. I'll help you look after Fred, we'll cheer him up. Annie, I'm sorry about this week, sorry about everything. I've handled it all so badly."

She could see that he thought this was all it would take. He had not understood the events of the past week in any way that assimilated the fundamental life changes that had occurred for her. "It's not that easy, Louis."

She felt the deeply familiar compulsion to look after him, protect him from these things she was about to tell him, things that might destabilise him. She tensed her calves and pushed her feet firmly against the floor. She had a sudden flash of sensual memory; the feel of Matthew's skin naked against hers, the smell of him. She knew that her attraction to him was somehow very different to the way she had felt attracted to Louis, for she also wanted the other things he offered her; gentleness, kindness, consideration, trust. Things that had been missing in her life and that she now yearned for more than anything. She sat up as straight as she could in the low chair. Her voice was steady. "I looked at an apartment today. I'm going to put an application in for a six month lease. That should give us time to sort things out."

"Sure, babe, if you need your space for a bit. I'm away for a couple of months out of that time anyway. Just as long as we find a way to sort it out, it's fine with me."

"That's not what I mean, Louis. I'm leaving you. I want this to be over. I can't be this way any more. I can't stand the way we are together. I don't like who I am with you."

He stared at her in frank disbelief. "Annie, you can't give up on us. We've had seven years together, a life, a baby. What is this about, some guy you knew in your teens? What has he got to do with all we've been through together?" His voice was quivering with emotion. He leant forward on the couch, his hands on his knees. She knew this place. Any moment he could be on the ground in front of her, his head in her lap.

"When you left here yesterday morning you sounded pretty certain we were over." Her voice was steady.

"Look, those things we said, they had to be said. You've been right all along. We had to talk about him, about Anton." It was the first time he had ever said the name. His eyes and voice were full of yearning. "Stay with me, Annie, forget the stupid flat. We can make this work. We can make another baby." He laughed suddenly. "Maybe we already have, hey, what about the other night when you came back from the hospital?"

Anna felt a wave of revulsion surge up inside her. "If that's the case, Louis, you can have visiting rights."

"You fucking vicious bitch! I can have visiting rights! That's what I get for trying to reach something that might resemble a heart in you?"

She looked at him coolly. "I'm sorry, Louis. It's too late. It's over. I want something different to this."

"Yah, well don't come crawling back when lover-boy's had enough of you."

"What about all those one night stands you've had recently?"

"Recently? You can't really be that naive! I thought you knew they came with the territory, that you were fine with it as long as we didn't mention the subject." His eyes bored into her, mocking her, full of hatred.

For an instant she was sure that she had in fact gone mad. She used every bit of willpower and restraint that she had to stop herself from flying at him, for she had an overwhelming urge to gouge his eyes out. But then she would be just like her mother, not to mention a probable trip to jail and the loss of medical registration. Her rational side won out in that instant and all he was aware of was a strange flicker in her eyes.

ACKNOWLEDGEMENTS

With thanks to:

The Royal Women's Hospital, Melbourne.
My daughter Natasha for offering me her favourite quote when
I was searching for a title.

ABOUT THE AUTHOR

Pauline Schokman was born in Sri Lanka and as a child migrated with her family to Australia in the mid-1960s. She is a general medical practitioner who practiced for more than a decade before training as a psychoanalytic psychotherapist, a field in which she has worked for over twenty years. She lives and practices in Melbourne.

9 781912 573639

Then my alcoholic haze was interrupted. A seven-foot-tall hairless, beige humanoid was harassing Sasha. He was leering over her, tossing money at her and insulting her honor.

"Slut. Whore. Harlot," he taunted.

Sasha ignored him as best she could and continued sipping her drink. The rest of the bar turned quiet. All eyes were on the drama unfolding between the two of them. Finally, he got her attention. She turned around looked him up and then down. It took quite a while due to his height. When she was done, she looked him in the eye and yelled, "Ha!" She returned to drinking and ignoring him. He was enraged. From behind, he grasped her in a headlock.

Before I knew what was happening, someone had tapped him on the shoulder and told him to "Leave the lady alone."

To my surprise, I realized it was me. He turned around. Then down. He looked me over quite quickly and laughed in my face. I could hear Kerr yelling "Go get him, Dirtling!"

"Just leave and we won't have to resort to violence," I said. He did, in fact, let go of her neck but only so he could get a punch at me. My reflexes took over like they had in the diner. I ducked and swung. My punch connected despite the fact that my eyes were closed at the time. My opponent flew across the bar and his back was slammed into a wall. A second later, he slid down to the floor unconscious. In Tore's lighter gravity my punch had real power. I stood there shocked.

My shock soon turned into pain as something hit the back of my head. I staggered around to see the remains of a broken chair in the hands of another humanoid just like the first. He threw a punch at my face, hitting my right eye. My reflexes seemed to have taken a coffee break but that didn't mean I was out of ideas on how to defend myself. I continually pummeled his fist with my face and it felt like I was beginning to wear him down.